SPOOKABLE TALES VOLUME 2

LOUIS PAUL DEGRADO

Louis Paul DeGrado

**Spookable Tales Volume 2
Copyright © 2020 Louis Paul DeGrado**

All rights reserved. No part of this book may be used or reproduced by any means, graphic, electronic, or mechanical, including photocopying, recording, taping, or by any information storage retrieval system without written permission of the author.

This book is a work of fiction. Unless otherwise noted, the author makes no explicit guarantee as to the accuracy of the information contained in the book. Any reference to people or places that may be real is merely coincidental. Just in case the characters in the story come to life, you should beware and lock your door at night.

Also Available from Author Louis Paul DeGrado:

Savior

The Round House

The People Across the Sea

The Questors' Adventures

The Calling of the Protectors,

The Legend of Chief

The Calling of the Protectors,

The Mighty Adventures of Mouse, the Cat

The 13th Month

13 Days

Spookable Tales Volume 1

Anna's Art Center

Anna's Art Center Book 2, Rules, Chores and Cookie Batter

Louis Paul DeGrado

www.Literarylou.com

Special Thanks goes to:

Kyle and Kendra Groves
Kathleen Mack Groves
Ed Groves
The Party People Theatre of Mystery

Louis Paul DeGrado

Special mention goes to the Cast and Crew that Made *The Vampire Detective* **come to LIFE:**

Drake Ulah - Colin Stewart
Lacie Starlight - Lexi Deary
Bob - Matthew Coats
Veronica Charm - Martha Page
Freddie Flicks - B Kevin Ritter
Adam Staulker - Jeffery Orman
Director - Pam Kramer
Tech - Caleb Miessler

Gather Around

though you may despair

there's a tale of terror

in the air

Come not if you are faint of heart

For you might not last

But may depart

Not standing

but lying still

If adventure is what you desire

Then come closer

sit by the fire

And listen well

To the tale I tell

Louis Paul DeGrado

GRAVE ROBBERS

CHAPTER ONE
GRAVEYARD SHIFT

No one could explain what was happening all over the country, all over the globe for that matter. That's what the chief said. Hundreds and sometimes thousands of bodies had just vanished from cemeteries without a trace; the coffins left behind. The scale of the operation would have to be enormous yet, no one had seen or heard anything. That's how the briefing went.

Now, it's Friday night in Canyon City Colorado, and Jeff Denton is just arriving at his post at the Mountain Valley Cemetery. After retiring five years ago from his full-time job, Jeff settled in the town and started working part-time at the Canyon City Police Department; a job that has him working most weekends. Jeff takes out his lunch box and opens it. He puts a cold cut deli sandwich on the seat beside him and pulls out a thermos of coffee and pours himself a cup.

"It's going to be a long night," Jeff says to the empty car. He looks down at his sandwich and considers he would rather be off doing something fun, or at least eating a good pizza at the local joint and having a beer. Instead he is parked outside the cemetery watching for graverobbers. He remembers what led him to this point: The chief called him in. The Chief called everyone in. They were taking extra shifts due to a tip that a group of people digging up graves throughout the country were now in this location and could strike. Although the cemetery had a night guard, the chief thought an extra set of eyes wouldn't hurt.

Jeff positioned his vehicle along the south road that ran parallel to the cemetery. From here, he could see any vehicles approaching from the town below. He started thinking about the reasons someone would want to disturb graves; reasons that ranged from recovering or stealing family heirlooms to digging up buried treasure.

Jeff faded off in his investigative daydream when suddenly, his car started shaking and he sat up straight. "What the?" He shook his head making sure he wasn't dreaming. It was then he heard a low moan coming from outside his car. He reached for his flashlight and readied his weapon. The car stopped shaking but the moaning continued. He turned his head left and right and then rolled the passenger side window down.

It's coming from behind me, he thought as he readied himself to exit the car. He quickly pulled the door handle and stepped out of the car switching the flashlight to his left hand as he reached for his sidearm with his right. Standing about six-feet tall, Jeff was not a small man but had thick arms, broad shoulders, and a body-builders chest. His physique helped him get the job because no one usually messed with him. He took a step toward the back of the vehicle where he heard the sound. The moaning stopped and a faint whisper came from the rear of the vehicle.

"Jeff, Jeff Denton..." the voice called out.

It concerned him that whatever he was facing knew his name. He took another step and could see over the trunk, but nothing was in view.

"Jeff, Jeff Denton, ghosts cannot be shot," the whispering voice called out.

"Alright there, whoever you are come out and put your hands where I can see them!" Jeff commanded. "If one of you guys came out to prank me, this isn't the time."

"Jeff, ghosts cannot be shot, but humans can. Don't hurt the humans, especially one who is an old friend."

Jeff's trained eye spotted the figure as it stood with hands raised and he laughed. A fit man with red hair and blue eyes, dressed in a black coat and jeans grinned at him.

"Louis, what are you doing here?" he said recognizing his friend from Pueblo that he had worked with years ago.

"I should ask you that. Why are you parked outside of the cemetery? Are there some kids daring to go in?"

"No," Jeff said. "We had a warning about some grave robbers. Apparently, there's been a rash in Colorado and some towns in the area have been hit so the chief is worried we might be next."

"Oh," Louis said. "Well, it would be the perfect night for it;" he looked to the sky. "Overcast and chilly. Most people are probably staying indoors."

"Exactly why are you out here?" Jeff asked again. He knew Louis didn't live in Canyon but down the road in Pueblo.

"Research," Louis said. He reached down and picked up a small backpack. "Let's have a seat and I'll tell you what I know."

The two men returned to Jeff's car with Louis taking a seat in the passenger side. Louis took out a thermos and poured some coffee in a cup and handed it to Jeff.

"Thanks," Jeff said. "I have my own." He held up his thermos.

"First, let me apologize for the funny business back there," Louis said. "I just couldn't resist. You should have parked your car where you could watch the back more readily."

"I didn't expect anyone from that direction," Jeff said. "The cemetery is only six acres and has limited access. It's over there I'm watching," he points to the cemetery.

"All those trees don't help," Louis said.

'No, but I figure if someone is coming, they would probably be coming from the south and this is most concentrated part."

"Lots of places to hide out there," Louis said. "I really am sorry."

"Don't worry about it. You sneaking up on me is actually helping me stay awake. Got my adrenaline pumping. You still haven't told me what you are doing out here."

"I'm in town for a ghost hunt at the Abbey tomorrow night. I'm staying with Scott Holiday."

"Oh, how's he doing?" Jeff said. He and Louis worked in the same company with Scott five years ago.

"He's still stubborn as ever. Even with his share of that lottery money he won, he still won't leave his old house or go travelling anywhere. Just kind of sits home on his porch and makes fun of his neighbors that have to go to work."

"That sounds like Scott," Jeff said. "It would be nice to retire early and not have to work. What about you? You said you were doing research. Is the ghost hunt what you are researching?"

"Somewhat," Louis responded.

"You're still writing books?" Jeff asked.

"I am working on some new material," Louis said. "It has a supernatural flare. The ghost hunt is more of a hobby though. You'd never guess who is leading the group."

"Is it Joe?"

"How did you know?" Louis asked.

"Joe Durant, for all his technical mumbo jumbo and hard knocks approach, is one of the most popular ghost hunters in the area currently," Jeff said.

"They invited me out, so I decided to pay them a visit," Louis said.

"They?"

"Joe is leading the tours, but Mari Valdez is the one doing all the marketing and videos. She's the one that contacted me."

"Really," Jeff said. "I didn't know they were into that sort of stuff."

"They weren't back when you worked with them. But they started reading all my stories and watching my posts and next thing you know they are hooked on all that is spooky and supernatural."

"Why are you out here," Jeff asked. "At the cemetery?"

"I'm here for the same reason you are."

"The graverobbers?"

"Yes," Louis said. "Are all the cemeteries being watched?"

"Yes," Jeff said.

"And you are by yourself?"

"There's only so many of us. It's normally a quiet town," Jeff said. "That is until some hoodlums decide to come and tear up graves."

"There's more to these graverobbers than you might know," Louis said. "They aren't some young pranksters you're dealing with."

"No?"

Louis shook his head. "It's more sophisticated than you might think."

"How's that?"

"Tell me what you know and then I'll fill in the gaps," Louis said.

Jeff looked out his windshield and around the surrounding area. "I guess no one told me we had to keep this a secret or anything and it has been on the news. So, here's what I know.

"The chief pulled us in to a meeting and told us about this group of people that were going around digging up graves. Supposed to be going on all over the country. They've hit several towns in Colorado. We had a tip that they were in the area so, we've all been taking shifts and watching the cemeteries."

"Did he tell you if they were stealing anything?" Louis asked.

"That didn't' come up," Jeff said.

"Did he say if they were removing the bodies?"

"Just said that the bodies went missing without a trace."

"Are they digging up specific bodies newly buried or old?" Louis kept questioning.

Jeff shook his head. "We didn't talk about any of those things. All I know is it's illegal to exhume a body without the permission of the family or some type of court order. I guess that's enough for him to put me out here. Now enough with the questions, what do you know, and do you want some of these shortbread cookies my wife made or not?"

"Sure, I'll take some," Louis said.

Jeff took out the cookies and handed some to Louis. He dunked one in his coffee and ate it.

"These sure hit the spot," Louis said. "You know your chief has put you in danger. This thing is much bigger than they let you know. In fact, if I were you, I wouldn't feel safe being out here by myself."

"I don't believe in ghosts and spirits," Jeff said.

"That's not the problem," Louis said as he took a sip of coffee. "This is what I know. There is a someone responsible and they are real."

"They?" Jeff asks.

"Yes, they," Louis responds. "There's more than one and they travel in large groups and seem to be on a schedule when they do strike, in and out in a few hours like a well-coordinated plan. It could have something to do with the fact that they are trying to remain undetected. Anyway, this is more than some high school kids playing a prank."

Jeff suddenly looked past Louis to the cemetery.

"What is it?" Louis asked.

Jeff spotted a figure moving off in the distance. "Hold that thought," Jeff said. He opened his door, grabbed his flashlight. "I need to go check this out." He noticed Louis looked at the time. "Did you need to be somewhere?"

"No, I can wait," Louis said and got out of the car. "What did you see?"

"Over there," Jeff pointed. "Someone is walking over there."

"Let's go," Louis said and started walking to where Jeff pointed.

Jeff quickly overtook Louis and turned around to face him.

"If you get hurt, I'm going to get in trouble, now let me go first," Jeff said.

Louis started following him and Jeff turned around. "Not so close." Louis raised both hands palm out in front. "Okay, I'll stay back."

The two men slowly headed into the cemetery where Jeff spotted a figure lurking. Jeff knelt and watched but the person he was following moved slowly as though looking for someone.

"Maybe I should call this in," Jeff said.

"You think we're in danger?" Louis asked.

"No, I think we're okay. There just appears to be one person. He is acting suspiciously, sneaking around like that. Come on, let's get closer."

The figure, dressed in work boots, a large grey flannel jacket and black cap, moved deeper into the cemetery and eventually stopped at some tombstones and crouched behind them while looking forward into the center of the cemetery.

"Time to find out what you're up too," Jeff said and pulled out his flashlight. "You there, halt."

The high beam startled the man in front of them as they came up behind him. He turned and immediately raised his hands.

"Scott?" Jeff said.

"Jeff?" the man in front of him said as he squinted.

Jeff turned off the flashlight and he and Louis approached a man that had brown hair, a mustache and beard who they both knew as Scott Holiday.

"I thought you were staying with him," Jeff said to Louis.

He is," Scott said. "That's why I'm out here. When he told me what was going on, well, I figured I better get out here and look at the family plot. You know, to make sure it's safe."

"Okay, Louis, now that we've discovered who our mysterious stranger is and that he's not a threat, why don't you finish telling me what you know," Jeff said.

"A few years back, "Louis said, "I stumbled on this group. They called themselves the serenities. At first, I thought it had to do with an old television series I liked so, it piqued my interest. Once I got past the introductions, I found out a lot more."

"This isn't one of your stories is it?" Jeff asked knowing that Louis was an author.

"No, this will knock your socks off and has everything to do with what you've been hearing and more."

"I should probably drive around some," Jeff said.

"I don't know," Louis said. "You have a fairly good view from here. Besides, what I'm about to tell you is barely believable."

"Okay, okay, go ahead," Jeff said. "Let's walk up to the boundary there and back."

The three men started walking as Louis continued telling them what he knew. "These grave robbers that you are talking about, you do know it's much larger than Colorado? In fact, it's a worldwide phenomenon and has only increased over the last decade."

"Really, a decade?" Jeff said. "I hadn't heard about it until recently."

"Yes. Hasn't gained attention because it's not like they are killing people, right? The cemeteries have stopped reporting it because it's an embarrassment to them."

"I guess that could be bad for business," Jeff said. "So, why did it become so important that my chief wanted me out here?"

"People get upsent when someone disturbs their loved ones that have passed on," Scott said.

"Right," Jeff said. "Louis, you don't think what is going on is a prank?"

"That's what I'm getting too, but first, I need to let you know more about this group I met."

"Online?"

"Yes, online."

"Shh," Scott said raising his finger to his lips. "I hear something."

Everyone went silent and the flashlights went off as they came to a halt. Jeff went down on one knee and the other two did the same.

"I don't hear anything," Jeff said.

"That's because you don't have these," Scott said and pointed to hearing aids on his ears. "See, I had to invest in these."

"I hear it too," Louis said. "There's some rustling over in that direction."

Jeff stood causing Louis and Scott to stand. "I guess I can't convince you two to stay behind."

"Nope," Louis said.

"Not a chance," Scott said.

"Okay, just stay behind me," Jeff said and cautiously moved toward the area where Scott indicated hearing rustling sounds.

He glanced at Louis, who shrugged his shoulders, and unholstered his weapon before continuing forward.

Suddenly, Jeff took a knee. Scott and Louis slowly came up to him both in a crouched position. Jeff looked forward and pointed. "Over there, two figures just ducked behind those big tombstones."

"Just two?" Louis asked.

"That's all I saw," Jeff said.

"Your hearing might not be good, but you have excellent eyesight," Scott said.

"I had that Laser surgery a few years back," Jeff said.

"I'm glad we are catching up on how old we all are and all the medical procedures we've been through," Louis said, "but shouldn't we be keeping it down? Anyone out there is going to hear us and know we're coming."

"Right," Jeff said. "Stay behind me." Jeff proceeded slowly with Louis and Scott in tow. As they approached closer to the large tombstones all three of them could hear a man and a woman speaking in hushed voices. They could also see light flashes coming from what appeared to be someone checking a cell phone.

Jeff reached for his walkie talkie.

"What are you doing?" Louis asked.

"I'm going to call the station," Jeff replied. "Even if these aren't the people we're waiting for, they are in the cemetery past curfew. I'll probably just scare them off but in case something develops, I want the station informed."

The voices grew louder, and Jeff saw Louis cock his head toward them and then he put his hand across the walkie talkie before Jeff could make a call.

"Wait," Louis said. He took his cell phone out and dialed a number.

From in front of the three men, behind the large tombstones a ringtone from a phone sounded; retro seventies dance music played, and a male's voice could be heard.

"Oh, crap, I forgot to turn my cell phone off," the male voice said.

The tone went off and Louis' call didn't go through. Jeff watched as he hit the redial. This time the caller picked up.

"This is Joe," a hushed voice came from the other side of the tombstones.

"Joe, this is Louis, where are you?"

"I'm, uh, at home of course. Where else would I be at this time of night?"

Louis turned to Jeff and Scott and smiled.

"Just wanted to make sure we are good for tomorrow night," Louis said.

"No problem," Joe said. "The drums will be playing at the Abbey, it's a highly active site. You'll be amazed."

"Okay, see you then," Louis said and put away the phone. "You ready to have some fun?" Louis explained to Jeff and Scott what they were going to do. Scott and Louis took small flashlights out while Jeff stepped forward and slowly moved around the tombstone.

"NOW!" Jeff called out and Louis and Scott, flashlights blazing, flanked two people sitting on a blanket. "Don't move!"

CHAPTER TWO
REUNION

"Mari, Joe? What are you two doing out here?" Jeff asked as a man and woman, both dressed in solid black, stood in front of him.

The man, about five foot nine, stocky with short, black hair, and woman, five-five with long black hair were standing amongst a few backpacks and a cooler, lid open, full of ice and beer.

"We heard about what was going on," Joe said while he used a napkin to wipe his shirt from the drink he spilled.

"Is that all that is going on?" Jeff asked.

"Put your light down," Mari said.

Louis turned his light off while Scott pointed his to the ground. "Sorry," Scott said. "Didn't mean to make you spill your drink."

"We are just business partners," Mari said. "Our spouses don't like all this ghost hunting stuff and if it wasn't for, wait, Louis?"

"Yep it's me, and we knew it was you," Louis said. "Well, we knew it was Joe from his ring tone. I though you said you were home?"

"Very funny," Joe said and threw the napkin at Louis.

"Don't you have a ghost hunt at the abbey or something going on?" Jeff asked.

"That's tomorrow night," Mari said.

"What are you doing out here?" Jeff asked.

"You heard, didn't you?" Louis asked.

"We heard about the graverobbers," Joe said. "Wait, is that Scott? Scott Holiday?"

"Hello Joe, Mari," Scott said.

"Isn't this just one big reunion," Jeff said shaking his head. "At least I have back up if I need it."

"Funny we are all out here late at night compared to what we used to do; get up at the crack of dawn and go to work," Scott said.

"Oh, I'm sure glad I don't have to do that anymore," Mari said.

"Is there anyone else that's going to show up?" Jeff asked.

"Not that I know about," Joe said.

"Now that we're all here, what do we do now?" Scott asked.

"Looks like Joe and Mari picked out a good vantage point," Louis said. "Why don't we stay here."

"Okay," Jeff said. "But keep the voices down, I have a job to do out here."

"What's that?" Mari asked.

"They sent him out here to stop the graverobbers," Louis said.

"What do you know about them?" Jeff asked.

"Not much," Joe said. "All I know is that they aren't really grave robbers; they don't take anything. They just dig up the bodies and rebury them without the casket. It's some type of re-bonding with the earth or something like that."

"Sounds like a cult," Jeff said.

"Did you see the speakers?" Mari said.

"Speakers?" Jeff said.

"It's getting dark out and you probably missed them. Dozens of large speakers are along the perimeter pointing toward town."

"Why would someone have speakers out here?" Jeff asked.

"Want a beer?" Joe asked.

"I'll take one," Louis said.

"Me too," Scott said.

"I'm on duty Jeff said."

Everyone settled down on the blankets Joe and Mari laid out. The lights from the cemetery and city below bounded off the clouds creating and eerily clear visibility across the macabre landscape.

"Looks like it might rain before the night is over," Jeff said. "Louis, why don't you continue telling us what you know."

"Okay, I was telling you about this group that is responsible for all of this. You see, they believe in this energy force that makes up the earth and spirit of the earth; that all energy is life and all life is connected. Energy transforms, it doesn't really die. Humans are born of the elements. Those elements must return to the whole or the whole becomes weaker. In this case, the whole is the earth."

How did you get mixed up in all of this?

"That's the amazing part," Louis said. "We all know one of the leaders of this group, cult if you want to call it that. All of us worked with him!"

"Who?" Jeff asked but Louis didn't have time to respond before the entire cemetery went black. Every lamp and every light went out all around them.

"Do you feel that?" Jeff said.

Louis nodded.

Everyone in the group stopped talking as a low vibration came from the ground. Dull green and blue lights came from the direction of the vibration. The speakers emanated a low hum, but that wasn't all that caused the sound.

"It feels like heavy equipment," Jeff said. He stood and the others followed. From the position they were at, they could see across to the north and east of the cemetery and it was there that they noticed movement. Six formations of black clad figures surrounding small tractors started coming toward them. There were six in each row bringing the total number of people they could see below them to seventy-two. Jeff spotted more on the flanks; all in black. He could see they held shovels and rakes.

"Everyone get down," Jeff said as they hid behind the tombstones. He drew his weapon and took a small set of binoculars from his utility belt as Mari and Joe started snapping pictures.

"Make sure your flash is off, so they don't spot us," Jeff said.

"I think they already have," Louis said as he pointed to a group of four of the black-clad figures only thirty yards away that were looking in their direction.

Jeff removed his pistol from the holster.

CHAPTER THREE
AN EARTHLY MISSION

"Do you have seventy bullets?" Louis asked.

"No, but it will only take one to show the others I mean business."

Louis put his hand over to the gun and pushed it down. "I don't think they will harm us if we don't interfere."

"Interfere with what?" Jeff asked. He moved to the edge of the tombstones and Louis followed as they continued watching.

"Look closely at what they are wearing, Jeff," Louis said. "And I don't mean the black jeans and hoods, I mean the advanced night vision goggles."

"You're right about one thing," Jeff said. "This isn't a group of high school kids playing a prank." Jeff went for his walkie talkie and Louis put his hand on it.

"Don't," Louis said. "They think they are running out of time to save the world. I don't know how many officers they have in that police department of yours, but they'll kill you and anyone else that comes to stop them. Believe me, I know."

"What do you suggest I do? Just stand by?" Jeff asked.

"Yes," Louis said. "Just watch. I promise you; they don't steal, and everything will be back to normal when they go."

Through the small binoculars Jeff carried and the amount of light from the workers before them, the group watched in awe as a coordinated operation took place before them.

What appeared to them to be spotters led and flagged specific gravesites. After this, four people would come in and plant a bladed machine that cut the grass out in a grid. The perfect grid was moved to the side. Then a small tractor came along with a conveyor system that pierced vertically into the site and slowly move out horizontally emptying the dirt efficiently into a bucket behind the machine.

"Those tractors must be electric," Joe said. "They're too quiet to be anything else."

"Look at how the blades on the conveyer just move into the ground and dig a hole so efficiently," Mari said. "Where did they get this stuff? It must have cost millions."

"Billions is more like it," Louis said.

The group watched as each of the six machines in their view stopped within minutes of each other. Four members of each group raised what appeared to be cross bows and shot a single arrow into each hole. The rope tied to the end of the arrow was used to pull and raise a coffin which was set to the side. The operator from the tractor came forward and each group knelt before the coffin as in prayer before they opened it, removed the body, and then slowly lowered it back into the hole without the coffin. The coffin was then lowered into the hole over the body and the dirt was put back in. Finally, the grass that had been neatly removed was replaced on top. The group of six people again knelt at the gravesite as though in prayer before moving to the next site.

Amazed, Jeff sat and watched as this process continued for the next four hours.

"I can't believe how efficient they work," Scott said. "Each time something goes wrong at one of the sites whether it's equipment or a digging problem, someone comes along, and the problem is solved immediately. It's..."

"Unreal," Mari said. "I thought our ghost hunts were strange, but this is something I could have never imagined. Maybe we should get out of here."

"They seem to be leaving us alone," Joe said. "Be ready just in case."

"They've already done fifty sites by my count," Jeff said. "And that's just what we can see in front of us. I can tell there's some more lights over there. They just put the bodies back under the coffin. Don't take anything or do anything to it."

"How could they have possibly got all of this equipment here?" Joe asked.

"I have a theory," Jeff said.

Several minutes passed by.

"You going to tell us?" Joe asked.

"Sorry, I was just noticing it appears some of them are leaving," Jeff said. "My theory is that they are using the train. Just two days ago, the Royal Gorge Railway had to shut down for a day. Multiple people reported there was another train on the track just west of here."

"Isn't that track used by the gravel company as well?" Mari asked.

"I supposed it could have been a coincidence," Jeff said. "However, it makes sense that when you consider the amount equipment out there along with the weight of it all, that they are using the railroad to move it around. This is way out of my pay grade."

"Oh no," Joe said. He slumped behind the tombstone. "Get down. There's a group of them gathering and looking our way. One of them is pointing in our direction."

"It's probably nothing," Louis said. "We've stayed put and haven't interfered."

"One of them is walking this way," Joe said.

A figure in a black cloak with night-vision headgear came up the slope toward the group and Jeff looked as close as he could with his binoculars. The person's hands appeared to be free of any tools or weapons. I noticed he's also limping as though he has a bad left leg. The figure stopped about six feet from where the group had been watching. Jeff and Louis stood. Scott, Joe, and Mari did the same so that they were all exposed to the person walking toward them.

The figure moved both hands to its head and removed the goggles and hood.

"Crage? Crage Bryant?" Jeff said. "What are you doing here?"

"Livin' the dream," Crage said. "Thanks for not interfering. It always makes it messier when the local law enforcement tries to interfere." He looked to Louis. "I see you made it."

"You knew about this?" Jeff said as he turned to Louis.

"Kind of," Louis said. "I've been researching the phenomena and well, Crage kind of invited me out to witness the event."

"Thanks for providing the distraction and keeping Jeff and us safe," Crage said.

"No problem," Louis said. "Thank you for letting us watch the ceremony. Hope you don't mind that I invited Mari and Joe along."

"Absolutely not," Crage said. "The more people that understand this whole thing, the faster we can accomplish our mission."

"Ceremony?" Jeff said.

"Yes," Crage replied. "What we are doing is very thought-out and sacred. Everything we are doing has a purpose."

"Which is to save the earth?" Jeff asked. "How? I don't understand."

"You don't believe in our cause?" Crage said.

"I'm not sure I do either," Scott said."

Crage turned and looked at the last few members of his group leaving.

"You have another cemetery to hit tonight?" Jeff asked.

"No, Crage said. "I wanted to make sure no one is waiting for me. We have to load everything and be out of here tonight."

"Speaking of that," Joe said. "How did you get everything here without people in the town noticing. I mean, even as quiet as the equipment was, it's still a lot."

"What do you know about hypnotism?" Crage asked.

Everyone glanced at each other and back at Crage.

"See, there are speakers placed all around the cemetery days ago that are emitting a soft hum that grew louder each night. It was a programmed frequency vibrating in a way that lulled the town to sleep."

"That just blows me away," Louis said. "How come we weren't affected?"

"You are in the perimeter, just like the rest of us," Crage said. "The sound is a very focused wave. Technology I don't even understand."

"I still don't get what you are doing," Jeff said.

"Let me ask you," Crag said. "Do you believe in the effects of climate change, see what pollution does, understand the effects development has on wildlife and the ecosystem?"

"Yes," Scott said. "I understand that I can't keep dumping my sewage in the same place without making a stink. I've got to clean it up somehow."

The group laughed together.

"Okay, maybe I'm coming off too strong," Crage said. "For a long time, people have been looking only at the exterior effects we have on the earth from the things I mention. However, we all know energy doesn't die, it just transforms right?"

"Yes, Louis reminded us what Einstein said; 'Energy cannot be created or destroyed; it can only be changed from one form to another.'"

"Exactly," Crage said.

"So, you think you are returning the energy to the earth by having those people rot in the ground instead of the coffin?" Scott asked.

"They decay and are absorbed back into the host." Crage said. "A complete absorption not possible with some of the casket designs of the day."

"Is there any proof of this?" Jeff asked.

"Sounds like some made up mumbo jumbo so that people like you have something to do when they retire," Scott said.

Crage smiled. "You'd be surprised who knows this is true," Crage said and pointed to the sky. "You think all those satellites they've sent into space are for tv and phones? There're devices up there that measure the earth's ionosphere, temperature, weather patterns and all kinds of stuff. They have the information. And they have data before and after we started doing this. They just don't understand how what we are doing works."

"How long do you think this will go on? How long before someone puts a stop to this?" Jeff asked.

"Oh, heck," Crage said. "We're just a small group and haven't been doing this long. There are seventy or more teams doing this just in the U.S. God knows how many there are worldwide. It will all come to a stop soon."

"How's that?" Jeff asked.

"New legislation will be passed within the next decade that will require all coffins to be made biodegradable," Crage said.

Really? Scott said.

"Yes," Crage said. "It's something we need to do anyway for the environment and space concerns. We can't just keep expanding cemeteries forever. You'd be surprised how high up this all goes."

"I guess then we will just have to worry about climate change and all the other bad stuff we are doing to the planet," Mari said.

The group shared a laugh.

"What am I supposed to tell them at the office?" Jeff asked. The moment he spoke, the lights in the cemetery came back on and as he looked around, there wasn't a soul present other than the group he was standing with.

"Nothing is missing, nothing's out of place. See those guys," Crage pointed to several guys dressed as landscapers raking the grass. "They are going to cover our tracks the best they can. Tell your chief that all you spotted was the landscaping service maintaining the sites."

"What if anyone reports the strange lights and sounds?" Jeff asked.

"Tell them," Crage pointed around to the others in the group, "that it was a group of paranormal investigators doing a ghost hunt."

Louis, Joe, and Mari laughed.

"This is going to make a great story," Louis said.

"It was sure good to see all of you," Crage said. After several handshakes, he walked away.

Suddenly, Jeff's walkie talkie went off. "Officer Denton, this is home base. We have reports of strange lights and sounds coming in from around the cemetery. Is everything okay?"

"I'm out here with some paranormal investigators, they're looking into it as well," Jeff said. "So far, all we've seen is the landscaping service doing their job. I'll keep you informed if I see anything. Over and out."

"It will be light soon," Louis said. "I guess we should get some sleep since we are going to have another late one tonight."

"That's right, we better get going," Mari said. "We still have some stuff to set up." With that statement, Mari and Joe parted.

"I noticed you left your car at the house," Scott said to Louis.

"I walked here," Louis said.

"Do you need a ride back?"

"I'll take him back," Jeff said.

"Okay," Scott said. "I'll try to keep it down this morning so you can get some sleep."

"I'd appreciate that," Louis said.

Jeff and Louis began walking back to the road where his patrol car was parked. "I never expected a night like this. You knew about this all along?"

"Not exactly," Louis said. "I had some information about it and Crage invited me to witness it. I'm going to write a story about it; all fiction, of course."

"Of course," Jeff said. "Why are you looking at me like that?"

Louis stopped walking. "You know, you should come to the ghost hunt tonight. It'll be fun and you'll get to see everyone again."

Jeff started walking, "no way, I've had enough excitement for the weekend and my wife would kill me if I'm out another night."

"Bring her along," Louis said.

Jeff and Louis entered the patrol car and headed down the road as the sun began to rise in Canyon City, Colorado. Deep in the earth, bodies decomposed and gave the essence back to

heal the energy that sustained the very life of the planet on which they were living.

THE VAMPIRE DETECTIVE AGENCY

I Fell in Love with a Vampire

BY LOUIS PAUL DEGRADO

The following story was written as a play and will be presented as such. You will be provided a list of characters for your reference. During the story, I invite you to immerse yourself in the experience. Imagine that you are seated in a theatre, the lights are low, you have your favorite drink, some salty popcorn, and someone special by your side. You listen as the play begins and the characters take the stage.

Enjoy…

PS, in the event you are part of a group that wants to perform the play, please contact the author, www.LiteraryLou.com

The Vampire Detective Agency Volume 1 Notes:

Characters Sheet

Drake Ulah (yoolah): Detective, secretly he is a vampire that is over five-hundred years old. He is tired of feeling like he doesn't accomplish anything and has decided to use his skills to solve cases. He feels like no one knows him or knows who he is and is often depressed. He has watched the world he knows change many times and been witness to the death of those he loved. He only goes out at night so he makes excuses of why he can't do stuff during the day. He transforms into a bat when he travels.

Drake dresses in suits and is a proper gentleman. He does not bite people or hunt any longer. He uses fake blood drives to get his supply of blood and is often drinking "juice" boxes (really blood).

Lacie Starlight: Movie star, shining actress but humble in her demeanor. She is in the prime of her career but feels like someone is out to ruin her career. The movie she has been cast in is not a great one. She is starting to tire of the glitz and glamour and longs for love and someone to settle down with.

Lacie dresses like a movie star-extravagant with hair done and make-up

Adam Stauker: Older gentlemen who looks and acts like a slimy salesperson. He is the agent that represents Lacie but secretly, he is stalking her and is infatuated with her. He dresses like a stalker and if he wears a tie, it's a very thin tie. He is creepy, shifty, and uses too much hair gel. He flirts with Veronica whenever no one else is watching.

Bob: Drakes Silent partner (you'll find out why) Bob is an older gentleman who just retired and is not so happy to be out of retirement. He's good at eavesdropping, spying, blending in without being noticed as he's carelessly stealthy. Bob is not happy about his current situation but usually has a jovial and pleasant disposition. When Bob gets upset, it causes poltergeist-like activity.

Bob is always in the same clothes throughout and never changes.

Veronica Charm- Actress and Lacie's understudy. Veronica knows she is worth more than her current position is allowing her to be. She is stuck in a contract but desires to get out. She flirts with Adam when Lacie isn't watching. She is smart, witty, sometimes sarcastic. She dresses upscale and wears silk gloves, necklaces, and really fits the part of a movie star although the has yet to make it big.

Freddie Flicks- (could be guy or girl cast in this role) Movie Director that is nervous and behind schedule. He is currently in a slump and his current project, a Vampire love-story, "I Fell in love with a Vampire" is not going well and had many delays. Freddie dresses in odd colors of checkered suits/short pants and bow ties.

On the set, the Special effects is over budget and the movie has experienced many delays. The market is overrun with vampire love story movies and Freddie isn't sure this one will make the cut. He frets that it might be the end of his career.

Setting: (Remember, Drake only out at night!)

Room 1- Detective Agency: Three chairs and a desk and a file cabinet. A phone on the desk and a bell to indicate the door has opened. Props or furniture in the office is antique as Drake has been alive for Five-Hundred Years!

Room 2- Movie Set: Make up chair with mirror, Director's seat and two other chairs for actors/Actresses. There should also be a table with candles, books, glasses, and a knife (retractable fake knife) in the middle of the set.

Room 3- The street which will be the audience area the players can interact in.

Louis Paul DeGrado

Scene 1: The Agency

SETTING: (The scene opens with our main character, Drake Ulah, moving a wooden sign inside the detective agency. The sign reads "Blood Drive Today Only. Inquire Inside." The agency is sparsely furnished with two high-back upholstered chairs on one side of a large dark-wood desk. On the other side of the desk is another high-back office chair. The outside door reads "Detective Agency." Drake stores the blood-drive sign and sits at his desk staring at the door hoping for his first client to come through it. His silent partner, Bob, is pacing around while Drake sits at his desk watching the phone and looking at the door.)

Bob: Don't you ever worry that someday someone will get suspicious of your blood drives?

Drake: Would you rather I suck the blood out of someone?

Bob: You did it to me?

Drake: And I am a reformed man. Besides, I could not do it, not these days with all the drugs, perfumes, after shaves and other sanitary issues. The Blood Drive allows me to screen for healthy donors; it's for a good cause after all, I am helping the community by solving cases.

Bob: How long can you keep paying for this office with no clients?

Drake: I've had five-hundred years to save. Plus, I have an extensive collection of antiques to sell if needed.

Bob: Well, I'd get ready to sell some more. Another day is coming to an end with no clients. Maybe we need to hit the street.

Drake: You know I have a sun-allergy.

Bob: Maybe more people would come if you started earlier instead of being open late.

Drake: But I do my best work at night. Besides, more crime happens at night. Lighten up, people just don't know about us yet. Maybe I should take out another add. Or use some of that social media stuff, Facelook or flighter.

Bob: You don't even have a cell phone, when are you going to join the modern age.

Drake: The modern age, (*sigh*). I miss the days when people had time to talk to each other. When lovers wrote letters that took effort and had meaning. I miss, (pulls out a tissue and wipes his right eye)

Bob: There, there, things will get better.

Drake: Does anything I do matter, does anyone care, is my heart alone again, is anyone there?

Bob: I'm here.

Drake: Be quiet, I'm reciting.

Bob: Ah, (puts his hands over his eyes and shakes his head.)

Drake: I cannot see the sun, I cannot feel the warmth of its rays

Oh, how hollow and cold are my days.

Bob: Like your heart.

Drake: Yes (Drake puts both hands on his heart) like my cold, barely beating heart. Have I nothing left to give? Have I no life left to live? What sign is there that I should go on? I hear no calling, I feel no warmth, I am, am...

Bob: Stop. You're depressing me. Why did you open a detective agency? Out of all the things we could have done, why this?

Drake: I've tried about everything: Doctor, lawyer, teacher, priest, executioner.

Bob: Executioner?!

Drake: Yes. The uniform helped hide my identity and the pay, well, let's just say I had all the blood I needed.

Bob: What were you before you became, well, you know.

Drake: A vampire? I was an inspiring playwright.

Bob: Oh, anything I would know?

Drake: You think Shakespeare did all of that himself? I waited tables and worked odd jobs to make a living. I never got anything I wrote on stage before, and then, well, you know.

Bob: You didn't answer my question; why the detective agency?

Drake: I've always wanted to solve crimes. Joining the police would bring too much attention. Especially now with all the background checks, fingerprinting and stuff like that. Speaking of that, look what I got. (Drake reaches into his drawer and pulls out a fingerprint kit as he stands and walks to the front of the desk. Bob comes over to see.)

Drake: Here, touch this glass. (Drake points to a glass and Bob puts his hand around it but does not lift it off the desk. Drake takes a brush out of the kit and wipes the glass. Then he takes out a magnifying glass and raises the glass looking it over but seems to be unable to find anything.)

Bob: No fingerprint, right? Imagine that.

(The bell rings. Bob opens and Lacie walks in. She notices Drake but cannot figure out why the door opened. She steps forward. Drake turns and looks at her while Bob stands holding the door open.)

Drake: Sorry, the blood drive was last week.

Lacie: Blood drive? I thought this was a detective agency.

Drake: Would you PLEASE close the door.

Bob: Yes, sorry, I don't want to let any light in. With your serious sun allergy.

Lacie: (Turns to shut the door but it is already shut, by Bob)

(Although Bob speaks through the scene, Lacie never acknowledges him)

Drake: May I help you?

Lacie: Oh, there you are. It's so dark in here. Are you the detective?

Drake: (Stands erect and walks around his desk, straightens his suit coat, and puts out his hand) Yes, I am Drake Ulah, Detective. And who do I have the pleasure of meeting.

Lacie: My Name is Lacie Starlight and I need some help.

Drake: (Takes Lacie's hand the old-fashioned way and kisses her knuckle.) Please have a seat.

(Bob and Lacie head toward the same seat and Drake heads Lacie off)

Drake: Please, over here. (Drake motions Lacie to the chair opposite and holds the back until she is seated. Bob sits and shakes his head as Drake takes a seat behind his desk.)

Drake: Now, how can I help you?

Lacie: I think someone is trying to KILL ME!

(Dramatic Music Sound)

Bob: Probably because you tried to take their seat.

Drake: (Ignores Bob) What makes you think that?

Lacie: I am on the movie set for "I FELL IN LOVE WITH A VAMPIRE."

Bob: That explains the Movie Star name.

(Drake looks in Bob's direction with a disapproving look, eyebrows lowered, and then back at Lacie)

Lacie: The movie has had many delays and problems on the set. Just last week, a stage light mysteriously fell at a spot where I was supposed to be standing. Yesterday, the male lead playing the vampire came to my dressing room to talk to me. While we were talking, he said he was thirsty, so I offered him a drink that was just delivered to my room. After he drank it, he fell dead!

Drake: Dead?

Lacie: Dead!

(Dramatic Music)

Lacie: The drink was poisoned! At least that's what the police have told us.

Bob: Sounds like we have our first case.

Drake: Yes, it does.

Lacie: Yes, it does what?

Drake: Oh, sorry. I mean it does sound like a case.

Lacie: Oh please, Mr. Ulah.

Drake: You can call me Drake.

Lacie: Drake, (Lacie reaches her hands across the table and grabs Drakes hands) Please, help me.

Drake: (Drake looks down at the hands touching, an expression of emotion and loss crosses his face.) I will have to check my schedule. (Drake opens an empty schedule book in front of him making sure Lacie cannot see the inside which is blank)

Bob: Schedule? What are you talking about? This is our first CASE!

Drake: Be quiet please.

(Lacie pulls her hands back as if offended.)

Drake: I'm sorry, I mean I'd be quite pleased to take your case. (Drakes stands) I am booked until tomorrow evening. Would that be soon enough?

Lacie: (Stands) We are back on the set tomorrow afternoon and shooting into the late evening according to our director, Freddie Flicks. I can let the guard know that you will be coming by.

(Drake walks Lacie to the door)

Drake: Don't worry, I can get on the set.

Bob: He can turn into a bat and fly right on in.

Drake: Don't tell anyone you've hired me. That way I can get a look around before anyone knows who I am.

(Lacie Nods)

Drake: I will see you then. And don't worry, we handle this kind of thing all the time.

(Bob snickers in the background as Drake gives him a dirty look and then turns to watch Lacie walk away. Bob gets up and opens the door while Lacie is looking down. She notices the door is open and is baffled)

Bob: Charming young lady.

Drake: I'll say. (Sighs)

Bob: Oh my, are you falling for your first and only client? Isn't that a conflict of interest?

(Drake returns to his desk and pulls out a leather bag and starts filling it full of detective stuff like his fingerprint kit, gloves, magnifying glass, and binoculars)

Drake: No. I am not investigating her, and she is not married. Now, get off that subject. What are your thoughts about the case?

Bob: I think based on what she said, someone may be out to get her. We just need to find out who and why.

Drake: Now that you mention that 'what she said,' I would appreciate it in the future if you don't speak to me while I am interviewing a client. It's disruptive.

Bob: I thought we were partners in this.

Drake: We are but, it's distracting, and I can't focus on the conversation I'm having with the client.

Bob: You know, I don't even have my own desk.

Drake: (Takes out a leather attaché and begins putting things in it like a magnifying glass, fingerprint kit, and some other odds and ends- adlib and have him put something funny in it like a rubber chicken or something like that)

Bob: Are you ignoring me?

Drake: No Bob, I'm just getting ready to go out on my first case. Maybe we can stop and look at desks on our way back.

(Drake stands, grabs a heavy black umbrella, and exits)

END OF SCENE

Scene 2: "I FELL IN LOVE WITH A VAMPIRE."

SETTING: ON the movie set of "I fell in Love with a Vampire."
(Drake is currently a bat and is flying around in the audience as the actor uses the bat prop. He lands backstage and stands, straightening out his suit. Bob appears beside him. They are on the opposite side of Lacie who is there along her understudy, Veronica Charm, and the Director, Freddie Flicks. Freddie is standing while Lacie and Veronica are sitting down.)

Drake: Bob, keep your eyes and ears open. Look around and see if you can overhear or see anything suspicious.

Freddie: (Freddie Flicks notices Drake on the set. And hurriedly walks toward him) Finally, you're here. I have been waiting all day for you. (looks Drake over) I guess you'll do but I would prefer someone taller and more, well, more fit in the upper body.

Drake: Pardon me?

Freddie: Do you have any experience playing the role of a vampire?

Bob: Does he? He's the perfect fit.

Drake: I thought I told you to look around.

(Bob smiles and starts walking around the area)

Freddie: Look around?

Drake: Sorry, I meant, I'm here to have a look around.

Freddie: Aren't you from the acting agency?

(Drake shakes his head)

Freddie: (puts a hand on top of his head and closes his eyes as though he has a headache. Then whispers) Are you the investigator from the insurance company?

Drake: Yes (raises his right hand with his index finger gesturing) I am Detective Drake Ulah, they sent me to investigate.

Freddie: I suppose you'll want to speak with everyone who was here on the set the day of the incident.

Drake: Yes. I need to speak to everyone who was on the set that day.

Freddie: Well, I'll have to round them up. Except for that guy (points to the audience.) He wasn't here the day it happened. I don't even know why he's here. Why are you here? (adlib, banter with audience)

Veronica: (Veronica has been listening to what is going on and finally stands to meet Drake) With the security these days, almost anyone can get on the set, I mean, do they look like actresses and actors to you (points at audience).

Drake: And you are?

Freddie: Let me introduce you to Veronica Charm. She's Lacie's understudy.

Veronica: (puts out her hand and Drake takes it and kisses her knuckle)

Drake: Charming name.

Veronica: Oh, Darling, it's such a relief to have someone down here from the studio's insurance company. I just don't feel safe here any longer. Do they have any idea who's responsible for the dreadful things happening around here?

Drake: (Stands Erect) That is what I'm here to find out.

Veronica: (Flutters her eyes) Oh, my. You sure you're not an actor with that profile.

Freddie: Gather around everyone.

(Everyone but Bob comes closer to Freddie. Lacie's agent, Adam Stauker, enters but stays back watching)

Freddie: This is Detective Drake….

Drake: Ulah

Freddie: (Raises an eyebrow at the unusual name as he says it) Detective Drake Ulah, sent from the movie studio's insurance company. He's going to ask a few questions and I want you all to cooperate.

(While Freddie is introducing Drake, Lacie raises her hand and Drake puts his finger to his mouth in a motion to have her remain quiet so she puts her hand down)

Adam: (Adam Stauker steps forward) An investigator? It's about time this studio does something. All these setbacks are setting back the career of my star actress. I demand some results!

Lacie: Please Adam (she stands and touches his shoulder as he turns and looks to her with lustful eyes) let this man, what was your name?

Drake: Detective Drake Ulah.

Lacie: Can we just let him do his job so we can get rolling again?

Drake: (Drake steps forward looking at Adam) You are?

Adam: I am Adam Stauker, movie star agent. Lacie is my biggest star.

Veronica: Ha! Falling star maybe.

(The outburst by Veronica attracts attention)

Adam: What did you say about my star?

Veronica: Oh, I mean, ha, look what I found, a shiny penny in my pocket that I didn't know was there. Isn't that good luck or something. (she takes it to Adam who is stern at first, but then raises an eyebrow at Veronica's flirtatious look)

Drake: I'll start my questioning with him. (Drake points to Adam as the rest take seats and Bob mulls around them. Drake takes a small notebook and pencil from his bag that he brought.) You are Adam Stauker?

Adam: Yes, I am.

Drake: Please take a seat (Drake sits in the Director's chair) What is your relationship with Miss Lacie Starlight?

Adam: I've been her agent since she started.

Drake: Have you noticed anything suspicious around here lately?

Adam: You're talking about the accidents? (Drake nods) This movie has been vexed from the start. The day we arrived on set, there was a fire. Then, one of the lights fell on the set and almost hit Lacie. If she hadn't moved offstage to fix her make up at that precise moment, it would have been over. I suppose you're here about the poison in Lacie's drink that killed her co-star?

Drake: Yes, I heard about it. Did they know what was in it?

Adam: It was a chemical mixture of several household items, all found around the set; mixed in a blend that was not bad to taste at first, but the aftertaste was, (pause and look toward audience) TO DIE FOR.

Drake: Interesting.

Adam: I would say there's something suspicious all right. (Leans in and lowers his voice) You know, Freddie's career has been in a slump.

Drake: If his career is in a slump, why would you let your number one star be in this movie?

Adam: (Dismissive) Everyone's doing vampire movies these days. It's almost a requirement to be in at least one.

Freddie has a lot to lose if this movie flops but a lot to gain if it doesn't get made. The studio has insurance on him and the movie. He gets paid even if it doesn't get made. Sounds like they don't trust him, and I wouldn't either.

Drake: How's that?

Adam: As the director, he has access to everything around here, know what I mean. I would start looking closely at Freddie Flicks.

(On the other side of the stage, Freddie is sitting and talking to himself while Bob listens)

Freddie: This movie is going to be the end of me. Sure, the studio will pay me off if it flops, even more if it doesn't get made, but then my career as a director is over. Why'd I ever let that magician Kyle Groves talk me into making a vampire movie?

Drake: Mr. Flicks, I'm ready for you.

(Freddie and Adam Change places.)

Adam: (As stands he whispers) Remember what I said, I'd look closely at Freddie Flicks.

Freddie: (Takes a seat) I hope this isn't going to take too long. We have a schedule to meet.

Drake: I've heard about all the suspicious stuff going on around here: the fire on the set, the light falling, the poison in the drink. That's a lot of strange accidents wouldn't you agree?

Freddie: No one told you about the notes and the flowers?

Drake: What notes? What flowers?

Freddie: Lacie found love notes and flowers outside her dressing room. We suspected Adam but the notes were never signed, and they were all anonymous deliveries.

Drake: What made you think it was Adam?

Freddie: One night, I heard arguing. Adam stormed out of Lacie's dressing room. After their fight, the notes and flowers stopped. That is, they stopped right up until the day before the poisoning incident.

Drake: (Taking notes) What happened then?

Freddie: Another set of flowers came but they were dead roses. I had the security guard bring them to my office instead of delivering them to Lacie. The note on it read, "If our love is dead like these roses and I can't have you, no one can."

Drake: No signature?

Freddie: (looks to audience and uses his hands palms toward audience) *Anonymous.*

Drake: Do you still have the note? I can check it for fingerprints or match the handwriting.

Freddie: Sorry, I didn't keep the horrible thing.

Drake: Lacie doesn't know about the last delivery?

Freddie: Heavens No. She was having enough trouble already and I needed to get this movie on track. (Freddie leans in closer) Did you know Adam took extra insurance money out on Lacie? I also know he studied Chemistry in college. If I were you, I would take a close look at Adam Stauker! I mean look at him. (Drake and Freddie turn and look at Adam) Studied chemistry. The drink was poisoned. He's always watching her like, like a Stalker!

(Drake and Freddie turn and see Adam up against a corner fixated on Lacie as she brushes her hair)

Drake: Is it true, Mr. Flicks, that you make more money if this movie isn't completed than if it is completed and tanks?

Freddie: (Pause) Please don't say that word.

Drake: "Tanks?"

Freddie: No, "Money." This movie is way over budget and now I need to cast a new lead for the vampire. And why would I want this movie to fail? Then my career as a director would be over.

Drake: Thank you for your time. I think we're done here. Miss Veronica Charm, would you please come here and take a seat.

Freddie: (Leans in one more time) Remember what I told you about Adam.

(Veronica and Freddie change places)

Drake: What can you tell me about what has been happening on the set.

Veronica: Mister Drake, if that is your real name, and if you are really an investigator, you would already know what is going on here.

Drake: (Eyebrows raised) I am an investigator and that is my real name. I suggest you cooperate and tell me what you know about all the accidents around here.

Veronica: Oh, I like a tough guy. Maybe we can get together later. (winks) Lacie Starlight is what is going on around here.

Drake: Lacie?

Veronica: Oh, yes. See, she is at the top of her career, darling. But the problem with being at the top is there is only one way to go from there. (Gestures by putting her hand up and then swirling it down like a falling plane) She knows this role will damage her career. Her agent over there, (gestures) Adam, hasn't got her best in mind. He's too hurt because she's spurned him. I have the same problem with my agents. Freddie over there (nods in Freddie's direction) has more to gain if this movie flops, which it will, terrible writing. They should have hired someone better for the writing like that up and coming Louis Paul DeGrado. Anyway, with all this bad mojo (gestures shaking both hands in the air in front of her), no one here really has a chance or desire to make this thing work. It's no wonder so much is going wrong.

Drake: Mojo? You think the set is cursed?

Veronica: Yes. With so much negativity on set well, sometimes I find it hard to breathe.

Drake: So, you think this is all bad luck and no one is out to hurt Lacie?

Veronica: On the contrary, darling, I think everyone is out to hurt her, including Lacie herself. She just doesn't know it.

Drake: Thank you Miss Charm, I think we are through. Just one more thing to ask you. What would you gain if this movie didn't make it or if Lacie was to have an unfortunate accident?

Veronica: I am under contract to be Miss Lacie's understudy. If she were injured, I would be the star of this awful thing. If it were cancelled, I would have to go to whatever project she would take next.

Drake: Thank you Miss Charm. Miss Lacie Starlight, you're next.

(Veronica rises from her seat but leans in and whispers in Drakes ear giving him full view of her neck. Drake's face is turned toward Audience and they can see him glancing and being tempted by her neck)

Veronica: (Whispering) I would be careful around Lacie Starlight.

(Veronica moves back to her seat as Lacie sits in the chair by Drake. Drake composes himself. Bob takes this time to walk over and listen in to the conversation)

Lacie: (leans in) You're working for the insurance company?

Drake: Of course not. It was merely a matter of mistaken identity that I went along with.

Bob: You better hope the real investigator doesn't show up and bust you.

Drake: It's all under control.

Lacie: Pardon me?

Drake: I mean to say it gives me the perfect cover to ask questions without bringing suspicion on you.

Lacie: Have you found out anything?

Drake: Plenty. Just go along with the questioning and we can get together later to discuss the details.

Lacie: (Raises her voice) Yes, detective, how can I help you?

Drake: How come you didn't tell me about the flowers and the notes?

Lacie: I didn't think it was important.

Bob: Maybe she didn't want you to know she had a love interest.

Drake: Who were they from?

Lacie: A secret admirer.

Drake: Not Adam?

(Bob looks toward Adam)

Lacie: I suppose it could have been him, but he never admitted it. He has been acting strange lately and there was that one night...

Drake: The night that you argued?

(Bob turns back to the conversation)

Lacie: Yes, how did you know that?

Drake: I'm an investigator, it's my job to find out what is going on.

Bob: Oh please, someone told you that.

Drake: Would you please be quiet.

Lacie: (Leans back as though offended and then leans forward and talks in a lower voice that Drake can't hear)

Drake: Speak up please.

Lacie: (Irritated) I thought you said to be quiet? Which is it?

Drake: Sorry, please speak louder.

Lacie: Adam would never hurt me.

Drake: Tell me then, is there anyone here who would benefit from you being hurt?

Lacie: Veronica has it in for me.

Bob: Ask her why. Veronica looks like she could go out and be a star on her own. Why is she Lacie's understudy?

Drake: Why Veronica? Couldn't she go out and make her own career?

Lacie: No. She signed a contract to be my understudy. Until I don't have a part, she doesn't have enough time to make a movie of her own. That's why I think we need to investigate her. When we started working together, she was so sweet and...

Bob: Charming?

Drake: That's enough.

Lacie: I'm sorry, are we done?

Drake: No, I mean, I think I've got enough information here. I'll see what I can find out. Until then, I'm going to study these notes and I'll get back to you tomorrow. (Stands) Thank you everybody. I have enough here (raises his notebook) to make my report.

Freddie: Okay people, let's get back to work. We have schedule to meet.

END OF SCENE

Scene 3: PUZZLING PREDICAMENT

SETTING: (At the detective agency the next day, Drake and Bob are discussing the case. Both are at Drake's desk looking over a pile of notes he took. They have a chart on a dry erase board, or something similar, listing the names of the potential suspects: Lacie Starlight, Adam Stauker, Freddie Flicks, Veronica Charm, Secret Admirer.)

Drake: (pacing, he looks at the notes and at Bob) What did I tell you about being disruptive when I am investigating? The whole time we were there you were a distraction.

Bob: I was investigating!

Drake: You kept talking to me.

Bob: What if I need to ask a question? It's not like they can hear me. I thought we were partners on this! I don't even have my own desk. (Bob is pacing again and appears upset. The glass falls off the table by itself and Drake picks it up and puts it back on the table)

Drake: The desk again? We are partners. Now calm down before you break something.

Bob: Break something? I wouldn't be here if it weren't for you.

Drake: Hey, not fair. How many times do I have to apologize? I was new. I didn't think I took that much blood.

Bob: You killed me!

Drake: For that you decided to haunt me? Why didn't you go to the light?

Bob: I don't know, I was upset.

Drake: And how come I am the only one that can see you?

Bob: When you die, you are given a choice: go to the light or remain behind.

Drake: And you remained as a ghost?

Bob: Yes.

Drake: But there are a lot of ghosts that many people see. How come I am the only one that can see you?

Bob: Oh, that's where it gets interesting. (Bob pulls out a brochure from his pocket, puts it in front of Drake) See, you have a choice; you can haunt a place like a cemetery or building, even a bridge or stretch of road. Then, you can appear to a lot of people.

Drake: I never knew. (Drake looks at the brochure in front of him)

Bob: The drawback is you can never leave; you are bound to that location.

Drake: I'm going to guess that's not what you did since you can move around.

Bob: (Bob puts his finger on his nose and points at Drake) I picked haunting a person. With that, you only appear to that person but, you can follow him or her wherever they go.

Drake: Lucky me.

Bob: Yes, lucky you. You already know about paranormal creatures and aren't even scared of me. My haunting is a waste and I'm stuck here. (Bob sits in his chair and starts crying) Death is so meaningless.

Drake: There, there. (comforts Bob) Although I'm not scared of you, you do annoy me quite a bit, does that count?

Bob: (Sniffling, Nods) That'll have to do.

Drake: I'm lucky to have you; you're the perfect silent partner. Especially for a detective agency.

Bob: (still sniffling) How so?

Drake: No one can see you. You can eavesdrop and no one will know you're there.

Bob: (Dramatic) NO ONE KNOWS I EXIST (starts crying again)

Drake: That's not what I mean. Look, you can enter places without being seen. We don't have to break and enter. I think we got a good thing starting here.

Bob: (Stops crying) You do?

Drake: I do.

Bob: And you are going to get me my own desk?

Drake: Yes, I will get you your own desk.

Bob: With a nameplate and all?

Drake: A nameplate, a chair, even a wastepaper basket.

Bob: What about one of those desk calendars? And a mug with some sarcastic saying on it?

Drake: Can we get back to the case now?

Bob: (nods yes and looks down at the notes Drake has on his desk) That's a lot of notes. Why didn't you use that power thing you do instead of asking all those questions?

Drake: You mean my power to Mesmerize? (strange music sound)

Bob: Yes, why didn't you do the old whammy so you could tell if someone was lying?

Drake: I wanted to do things proper. I am trying to improve my investigative skills. Tell me, what did you overhear?

Bob: Why do you have Lacie's name on the board as a suspect? Isn't she our client?

Drake: Something Veronica said to me made me think that she may be the cause of all of this, and she doesn't know it.

Bob: (looking at list) Freddie Flicks is on his way out. The past two movies he worked on tanked. He only took this one because he's out of options.

Drake: So, he is not a suspect (goes to board and starts erasing Freddie Flick's name)

Bob: On the contrary, he had the studio take out a massive insurance plan on the movie in case it doesn't go forward, they must buy it out. He gains more if they cancel it.

Drake: He's already lost his leading man, easy to replace as he was an unknown, but if he loses his star (Circles Lacie's name and draws a star by it and then write's Freddie Flicks name back on the board)

Bob: That's not all. I found scissors in Veronica's dressing room. I couldn't tell for sure, but it looked to have fibers on it. You know, like from cutting the rope the stage-light was hanging from.

Drake: She is wearing a wig for the set; it could have been fibers from the wig. But (puts his forefinger up and pauses in thought) she did mention that she was ready for a career of her own. Did you get any of the fibers?

Bob: No, but you can fly back there tonight and then we can compare them. Maybe Veronica is tired of living in Lacie's shadow. She is the understudy and Lacie herself was suspicious of her. Why are you underlining Adam's name?

Drake: (At the board underlining Adam's name) Lacie thinks Adam is harmless but he never takes his eyes off her. I've been alive for five-hundred years, I can spot unrequited love. There's nothing worse than a lover's scorn or in this case, a scorned lover.

Bob: Yes, but would it amount to Murder!

(Dramatic Music)

Bob: Maybe you suspect Adam because you are falling for Lacie Starlight, starbrite, kissy, kissy in the night. You should know better than to believe in love at first sight.

Drake: There is nothing more romantic. But what do I have to offer her...?

Bob: Oh no, here it comes. Come on, it's not that bad.

Drake: I suck blood.

Bob: So, I can't eat at all. You got a lot going for you; you are immortal, almost a god.

Drake: Not really, I can't eat stake (holds up the pencil in his hand and motions it towards his heart)

Bob: You have powers: Heightened senses of smell, taste, blood senses. You can tell if someone is lying, and you are exceptionally good at puzzles.

Drake: I cannot heal the sick or flood the world.

Bob: Okay, so maybe not a god but you can fly, and you have super strength. You're like, like, AN AVENGER!

Drake: Yes, that's it. A blood sucking avenger.

Bob: I'm trying to cheer you up.

Drake: I would be happier if we had a definite lead in this case. Right now, EVERYONE we've spoken too is a suspect. Including our client. (Drake circles all the names and then points to random audience member) Even that lady over there looks suspicious.

Bob: I think that's because she was sneaking extra snacks. Yes, I saw you. (points to her and nods his head)

Drake: (puts the markers down and sits at his desk) Oh, just admit it, we can't solve this case. (Drake puts his head down on the top of his desk. The phone rings)

Drake: This is the Night Avenger Detective Agency, Drake Ulah Speaking. (He winks at Bob excited with the new name he's created for the agency)

Lacie: (offstage, voice only) Drake, is that you?

Drake: Yes, Lacie, it is I. I just came up with that new name, what do you think?

Lacie: I think it is, uh, nice.

Drake: Thank you, now what can I do for you?

Lacie: I was wondering if you had any leads on my case.

Drake: (Looks at the board in front of him that's a mess and lies) Yes, we have several leads. I was just getting ready to call you.

Lacie: I'm down at the studio practicing my lines. It's just me here. Do you want to come by?

Drake: I will be there in a flash. (Hangs up phone, Whoosh, bat comes out and Drake flies to Studio)

Bob: (By himself he sits and examines his hands. He slowly notices the audience is looking at him and starts getting nervous. He stands and moves and notices people following him. Nervous laugh) Huh huh, wooo (spooky hands) and goes off stage.

END OF SCENE

Scene 4: A Horrible Accident

SETTING: (Back on the movie set Drake flies through the audience as a bat and then appears from the back of the set)

Drake: Good Evening, Miss Starlight.

Lacie: (Sitting and reading her script, she turns quickly, surprised) Wow, you got down here fast.

Drake: We are alone, no?

Lacie: Yes. We are alone, now we can talk. Did you find out who could be doing this?

Drake: (Approaches Lacie) As I said, we have some definite leads but not one prime suspect.

Lacie: We?

Drake: Yes, uh, I mean 'we' as in you and…I…as we are in this together.

Lacie (grabs his hands as she stands and moves close to him.) I was hoping you had better news.

Drake: It will be just a matter of days. It seems all of you have a reason to see this movie fail.

Lacie: What do you mean?

Drake: I'll explain. You think Veronica wants you out of her way so she can become the star.

Lacie: I don't know why she just doesn't leave? (breaks free and turns away from Drake)

Drake: She is bound by a contract to be your understudy. Unless something happens to you, she cannot be the star. And that's just the start. Freddie Flicks' career is hanging by a thread. The movie studio took out extra insurance on the movie in case it fails. He can make enough money to get out of the business if the movie flops. Of course, he denies he wants this.

Lacie: If Adam found out, well.

Drake: That's another thing, did you know Adam has doubled his insurance policy on you?

Lacie: (waves Drake's warning off as she turns) Oh, he has insurance on all his big stars. I wouldn't' worry about Adam. He's had an eye for me for a long time.

Drake: Oh, he has?

Lacie: Yes, but I would never mix business with pleasure. (She turns and looks longingly at Drake and steps closer to him) Not at my place of work.

Drake: Of course not.

Lacie: So, if everyone is a suspect, who is your prime suspect?

Drake: We are working on it, but it may take some more time.

Lacie: You said "we" again. What can I do to help?

Drake: Watch for anything suspicious and report it to me immediately.

Lacie: (moves to the table and picks up her script) I don't suppose you have time to help practice the scene I was reading. It's, a love scene. (she hands Drake the script. Bob appears.)

Bob: There you are. I haven't seen you fly that fast since, (puts forefinger to temple in thinking motion) Actually, I've never seen you fly that fast.

Drake: (Glances at Bob and raises his shoulders then turns back to Lacie) Of course I am willing to help. It may even give me insight to the reason someone might be trying to derail this movie.

Lacie: Do you have any experience acting?

Drake: Well, a long time ago when I was in France, I was a playwright and (Bob walks up and smacks him) No, no, not really any acting experience.

Lacie: That's fine. You are playing the part of the vampire, is that okay?

Bob: No problem, he fits the part. He can even do the flying bat scene.

Drake: Would you just stop!

Lacie: Pardon me?"

Drake: I mean, would you just stop right there where you are standing because the, uh, light is just glimmering down on you there.

Lacie: Oh, well, thank you. Here, take the script. I know all my lines.

Drake: (Takes the script and walks over to where Bob is standing to shoo him away. Lacie looks at him as he turns his motions into stretching his arms) Just let me warm up.

Lacie (Lacie closes her eyes as though meditating)

Drake: Is something wrong?

Lacie: No, just concentrating. This is how I warm up. Are you ready?

Drake: (nods. Both move to center stage around a small, round table that has candles, books and a tray of cheese and crackers with a knife. Lacie starts on the opposite side from Drake)

Lacie: I know what you are!

Drake: (Surprised) You know what I am?

(Lacie points to the script)

Drake: Oh, sorry. Give me just a second. (Drake turns his back to Lacie, clears his throat, silently reads the script, and then stands erect and turns around.) Please start again.

Lacie: Can you do an accent?

Bob: Uh, oh, here we go with the accent.

Drake: Accent?

Lacie: Yes, the vampire has a foreign accent.

Bob: Tell him why.

Lacie: It makes it more believable.

Drake: (Turns away from Lacie and grimaces and clenches his fists. When he speaks, it's with an accent for the scene) Very well. Let us begin.

Lacie: I know what you are!

Drake: No one really knows what I am, behind this, this, mask of a man.

Lacie: Everything you said to me is a lie, that is what I know. You've had many loves.

Drake: Yes, I have, you might as well know. How could I not have loved? I have been alive for five-hundred years.

Lacie: Two, it's two-hundred years. (points to script)

Drake: Sorry, two-hundred years. But none of them compared to you.

Lacie: I suppose they are all dead now.

Drake: Yes.

Lacie: Did you kill them?

Drake: Only for the sake of mercy, when they were sick, dying.

Lacie: Do you have someone now?

Drake: Not for a long time. I got tired of falling in love and watching it fade away. That is why you must understand how special you are for me to take that chance again!

Lacie: How could I love you? You're telling me you are a cold-blooded killer. (She puts her hand on his heart) See, no heartbeat. You have no soul. If you are dead, then be dead to me. (Lacie slowly moves around the table closer to Drake and grabs the knife on the cheese tray)

Drake: Yes, I am dead. But my soul aches for you. What can I do to prove my love for you?

Lacie: I want to know it's real. If you are already dead, this shouldn't hurt a bit! (She takes the knife and stabs Drake in the heart. The knife doesn't retract. Lacie tries to move it but its stuck) Oh, my, what have I done?

Drake: (Grabs the knife by the handle) Is that supposed to be a real knife? (pulls out the knife that is now full of blood and examines it)

(Bob rushes to Drakes side)

Lacie: We need to get you to the hospital!

Bob: Did she just try to kill you?

Drake: Don't be silly. You didn't know the prop was a real knife, did you?

Lacie: Of course not! It's supposed to be a prop and retract.

Drake: It's okay (pulls out a handkerchief and puts it over the wound) it didn't go very deep.

Lacie: (looks at the length of the knife and the blood noticing it must have gone deep) You are in shock; we need an ambulance.

Bob: Oh, don't worry about him, he's kind of impervious to stuff like that.

Drake: Shut up, would you.

Lacie: Beg your pardon?

Drake: Sorry, I mean, keep it down. We don't want anyone to hear us.

Lacie: Why?

Drake: This knife is supposed to be a prop, right?

Lacie: (nods) Yes, of course.

Drake: Someone must have changed it to set you up. Understand?

Lacie: No. I don't understand. Are you sure you are not in shock?

Bob: He's fine, barely bleeds at all.

Drake: Did anyone know you were going to be here tonight?

Lacie: I didn't tell anyone on the set. Other than the security guard outside, no one knows I am here but you.

Bob: And me.

Drake: (looks at Bob) Take a look around, would you?

Bob (exits)

Lacie: You want me to see if anyone is here?

Drake: No, stay here with me. From the script we are reading, you did exactly what you were supposed to do. It's my conclusion that someone has switched out the knife for a real knife.

Lacie: But why would someone do that?

Drake: If they can't kill you, they can frame you for murder.

Bob: (enters) Or she is a murderer. There is no one else on the set. You'd be the second lead man to die while working with her. Maybe the poisoning wasn't so...Accidental?

Lacie: (puts a hand to arm to her forehead in shock and nearly faints. Drake helps her to a chair)

Drake: It's clear someone wants you out of the way.

Bob: Or she (points to Lacie) is the murderer! But if you're right and you find the culprit, I'll admit you are a good detective and she's not a murderer.

Drake: And I'll say, "I told you so."

Lacie: What did you tell me?

Drake: I mean, don't tell anyone. What time are you shooting this scene tomorrow?

Bob: I wouldn't use the term "shooting" around here.

Lacie: Eight in the evening. Freddie wants everything shot at night just as it's supposed to be nighttime in the movie.

Drake: Good. All we must do is come up with a plan to find out who had access to the prop and then...

Lacie: Yes? (Lacie stands and comes close to Drake)

Drake: We expose the person who has been out to ruin your career!

Lacie: (Embraces Drake) Thank you! I feel safer already.

Drake: Should I escort you home?

Lacie: Don't you think you should get someone to look at that wound?

Bob: Oh no, it's probably already healed. Part of his vampire magic.

Drake: (raises his voice) Would you PLEASE (notices Lacie looking at him) not worry about me and have a great evening. I will see you tomorrow.

Lacie: Aren't you leaving?

Drake: I'm going to look around. You know, do some investigating before I leave.

(Lacie exits and Drake watches her)

Bob: (Sits down where Lacie had been sitting) Oh my, you really are hopeless. That scene you just did, it was too real for you.

Drake: Yes, Bob. Now I'm hopelessly in love. She really is like...starlight.

Bob: You know this can't end well; you will either suck her blood and kill her or outlive her and watch her grow old and die. Besides, she might suspect something when tomorrow you show up without stitches or any sign that you were stabbed IN THE HEART!

Drake: I am not going to dwell on that right now. If we don't find out who is trying to kill her or frame her, there won't be any Lacie Starlight left to worry about.

Bob: Okay. Remember, you are the second leading man that almost met a deadly fate. We need to be open to the fact that Lacie herself is a suspect.

Drake: Very well.

Bob: All the suspects should be here tomorrow except for...

Drake: Adam Stauker. We will have to call him and tell him that we have some information. That way he will meet us here.

Bob: That should get our suspects here. Except for, (delay) that guy! (point to random audience member and go closer to him) He looks suspicious and you know what?

Drake: What Bob?

Bob: I think he can hear me. (Get closer to the audience member) You know what else?

Drake: What Bob?

Bob: I think he can see me? (Speaks to Audience member) Do you see Dead People?

Drake: I hear Lacie's car in the lot. I must go now.

Bob: Where are you going?

Drake: I'm going to make sure Lacie gets home safe. I'll see you back at the agency.

(Actor playing Drake uses bat prop to fly around the stage and audience here)

Bob: (Addresses audience) Okay, now it's your turn to hear dead people. This is your chance to solve the mystery before the final scene. Take out your clue sheet and fill out who you think is the guilty party.

END OF SCENE and Audience Break

THE VAMPIRE DETECTIVE AGENCY WORKSHEET			
Who	Motive (why would they do it)	Supporting Evidence	

Scene 5: PREPARATION

SETTING: (Back at detective agency Drake is sitting at his desk looking at a picture of Lacie from a newspaper or magazine article)

Drake: Oh Lacie, you are my shining star, I wish to be with you wherever you are

Your heart is full of blood, fresh, warm, tasty blood. (clears throat) It warms my cool, lonely heart. Yes, I said lonely. (if audience doesn't respond with an "ahh" continue) Really Lonely. Really, really, LONELY.

Audience: Ahhh (hold up "AHHH" sign if needed to get response)

Drake: Thank you. People think vampire's suck. Well, we do, but we are just being who we are. It's a lonely life full of, well, loneliness. I can never relax or rest. Not truly. The world is full of vampire hunters and teenage seductresses with werewolf friends. It's never safe.

Bob: (Appears) Did you see anything last night?

Drake: I saw Adam Stauker

Bob: Lacie's agent?

Drake: Yes, he was outside in the studio parking lot. He followed her all the way home and then sat outside in his car most of the night. He got out of his car and started to go toward her window.

Bob: Let me guess, a bat flew by and he got spooked?

Drake: (laughs) You know me too well.

Bob: That's creepy. I bet you wanted too (Bob uses his fingers to make like a vampire fang going for his neck)

Drake: (pulls out a juice box, fake blood, and pokes a straw into it) You have no idea.

Bob: We still have no clear suspect.

Drake: Yes, but if Adam is stalking Lacie, he may be preventing anyone from getting close to her. I just need to prove my point.

Bob: How are you going to solve this case if you are so distracted?

Drake: Distracted?

Bob: Oh, Please. You are so infatuated with Miss Starlight (points to the magazine Drake was looking at). I knew she had you when you did the vampire accent rehearsing the scene. You know, the accent that every vampire has in every vampire movie that drives you CRAZY.

Drake: Yes, I know, Bob. Not every vampire has an accent. Some of us are from (insert your town name you want too here). But I didn't mind doing it with her.

Bob: How do you plan on drawing out the suspect?

Drake: By doing that scene again with Lacie. Whoever planted the knife will be watching, expecting the knife to be real.

Bob: Do they have a lead for the vampire part already?

Drake: They do now. (Drake picks up the phone) Freddie Flicks please. Freddie?

Freddie: (Voice only off screen) This is Freddie Flicks.

Drake: This is investigator Drake Ulah, we met the other day. Do you have a lead for the scene you are shooting today?

Freddie: No. Not yet.

Drake: (does accent when he speaks this line) Well, search no more. I can play the part and I have read the script.

Freddie: I don't know if we can find a costume in time. The original costume was still on the actor who, you know, died. We could probably do some make-up.

Drake: Don't worry, I have my own attire. One more thing, can you make sure that man, Adam Stauker is there to witness my performance.

Freddie: I will, dear, but you should know, Adam only represents certain types of stars. Those with, how would you say, a bustier profile than yourself.

Drake: Still, I would like him to be there. I will see you tonight.

END OF SCENE

Scene 6: An Accident? Or was it?

SETTING: (We are back on the movie set and Drake has convinced Freddie to let him stand in for the part of the vampire in the same scene he and Lacie were practicing the previous night. Freddie, Lacie and Veronica are on the set and Adam has been called)

Freddie: Okay everyone, take your places. We are practicing the love scene. Let's see if we can get through it tonight.

Lacie: How are we going to shoot the scene without a vampire?

Drake: (Enters with his vampire make-up and cape-he looks the part) I can fix that. (He walks over to Lacie who is speechless)

Freddie: Places everyone.

Lacie: (Goes to Drake and puts her hand on his heart where the wound should be, but he doesn't flinch) How?

Drake: I called Freddie last night. What better way to protect you than to be right here beside you?

Lacie: But you were wounded. I don't understand.

Drake: You will, in time. Just do the scene with me.

Lacie: (Low voice) You never go out at night. You appear out of nowhere, and you can't be killed.

Adam: (comes into view of the audience but stays back from the set)

Freddie: (Sits in his Director's chair.) Okay, everyone clear the set. Drake and Lacie should be the only ones in the scene. Let's roll! (cast still mulling around) I SAID CLEAR THE SET PEOPLE. We have a schedule!

(more panicked clearing as everyone, including Adam, steps out of the spotlight)

Lacie: (Closes her eyes as she did before when they were practicing and then opens them looking directly at Drake) I know what you are!

Drake: (Accent) No one really knows what I am, behind this, this, mask of a man.

Lacie: Everything you said to me is a lie, that is what I know. You've had many loves.

Drake: Yes, I have, you might as well know. How could I not have loved? I have been alive for five-hundred years.

Lacie: (Lacie doesn't correct him this time) I suppose they are all dead now.

Drake: Yes.

Lacie: Did you kill them?

Drake: Only for the sake of mercy, when they were sick, dying.

Lacie: Do you have someone now?

Drake: Not for a long time. I got tired of falling in love and watching it fade away. That is why you must understand how special you are for me to take that chance again!

Lacie: How could I? You're a cold-blooded killer. (She puts her hand on his heart) See, no heartbeat. You have no soul. You are, dead. And you are dead to me. (Lacie goes to the table and picks up the knife, hesitates, then turns to Drake)

Drake: Yes, I am dead. But my soul is alive, and it aches for you. (Eyes fixed on Lacie, he pulls her close to him and stares into her eyes,

STRANGE MUSIC, until she gets lightheaded and almost faints. Adam rushes to her side and sets her in a chair fanning her. Freddie runs up too.)

Adam: Lacie, oh, my Lacie what is it?

Freddie: Oh my, what next? Is she okay?

Lacie: I'm fine, Adam, Freddie. I just need some air.

Adam: (Stands, addresses Freddie) You are simply pushing her too hard. I insist that this thing be delayed.

Bob: (Comes up to Drake) Why did you do the whammy on her? Is this part of your plan?

Freddie: Oh no, what am I to do? (fretting with hands) We are already behind and over budget.

Drake (Nods at Bob) Can we continue with the understudy (nods toward Veronica) since we are so close to finishing the scene?

Adam: Well, I didn't mean for you to replace her?

Freddie: (Turns and looks at Drake) I don't see why not. Lacie can take a break. Veronica, you're on. (addresses Adam) Please clear the set.

Veronica: (Surprised) Shouldn't we wait and see...

Freddie: Come on honey, we're burning the midnight oil to get this scene ready.

Adam (disgruntled moves off and over by Lacie)

Drake: Don't worry, I'll help you if you need it.

Veronica: (Hesitant, Bob moves behind her and gives her a push, she looks behind her, as she moves closer to Drake)

Drake: You do know the lines, right?

Veronica: (Nods) Yes, I know the lines.

Drake: Let's go then.

Freddie: Take it from "What can I do to prove my love for you?"

Drake: (Nods and turns to Veronica. She doesn't have the knife so he places it in her hand as she is turned away from him) What can I do to prove my love for you?"

Veronica: I want to know it's real. (Turns to face Drake knife in hand) If you are already dead, this shouldn't hurt a bit! (She takes the knife and motions toward Drake but goes across his body without stabbing him.)

Drake: (Grabs Veronica's hand that holds the knife) You're supposed to stab me here. (As he pulls the knife toward him Veronica pulls back and drops the knife.)

Freddie: Okay honey, he was right, you're supposed to stab him. (claps twice) Come on, we simply must get through this scene!

Drake: (Grabs Veronica by the shoulders and stares, Strange Musical sound here!) Look into my eyes. You cannot lie to me. You are the one who cut the rope for the stage lighting?

Veronica: (in a trance-like state) Yes

Drake: (strange music again) And you are the one who poisoned the drink that was meant for Lacie?

Veronica: Yes, it was meant for her. No one else was supposed to get hurt.

Drake: And you were the one who switched the knife? It's real, that's why you couldn't do the scene.

Veronica: Yes, It's all true. She was supposed to kill you. Then she would be out of the way and I could be the star.

Bob: The only thing you'll be starring in is a rendition of Jailhouse Rock.

Lacie: (Stands and moves the chair to Veronica as she starts to collapse and sits down)

Veronica: (Twirling her hair, she has snapped) I just wanted to be a star. Like you (she looks at Lacie)

Adam: (pulls out cell phone) Get me the police!

Drake: I am Drake Ulah, a detective from the Night Avenger Detective Agency. I was hired by Miss Starlight to find out if someone was trying to hurt her. I have found the person responsible. (Turns to Freddie) Veronica Charm is guilty of murder and attempted murder.

Adam: Come on (he lifts Veronica out of the chair) the police are waiting out front. (Turns to Drake) Good work Detective.

Freddie: (Hands in the air) Yes, yes, good work Detective. Oh my, what's next, (follows Adam) this movie's going to be the death of me.

(Drake, Lacie and Bob are still on the stage and Lacie sits back in the chair)

Bob: They called you "detective."

Drake: Yes, they did. (moves over to Lacie)

Lacie: I'm sorry, what's that you said?

Drake: I was just saying, I guess WE solved it.

Lacie: (Nervously playing with her hands) Yes, WE did.

Drake: (kneels so he is level with Lacie) There's something I need to tell you.

Lacie: It's okay, you don't have to say it. (She turns away from Drake) There has been enough revealed today. Don't you think?

Drake: It seems you'll be safe now. Just be careful who you hire as your understudy next time.

(Lacie doesn't respond)

Drake: (Stands behind Lacie and reaches his hands out to touch her shoulders but doesn't) I'll send the bill to the studio. (Drake leaves with Bob comforting him)

Lacie: (Turns at the last moment to watch Drake exit. She stands and looks toward the audience and places her hands-on heart) Oh my, I think I'm in love with a vampire.

END OF SCENE

Scene 7: I FELL IN LOVE WITH A MOVIE STAR

SETTING: ("I Fell in love with a Vampire" Movie has come out. Drake hasn't seen Lacie in months. The Detective Agency is doing well, and Drake has had lots of movie star cases thanks to Freddie Flick's referrals. Bob is happy he has his own desk and is sitting at it trying to make an object move, a mug or something the audience can see. Drake is watching him and is buried in paperwork)

Freddie: (comes out and addresses the audience during the stage change) The movie was not the death of me. Lacie did such a good job, the movie was a smash. I was so happy with that detective, Drake, I sent all my producer and actor friends to him. (Pause. Nods head a few times.) I know, you're wondering whether Drake and Lacie ended up together. (goes to a random couple) Just like these two here who ended up together. How did you two meet? (doesn't let them answer but interrupts) Oh who cares, let's watch the rest of the play!
(Freddie Exits)

Bob: (staring at object/mug on his desk) I just don't understand it. I can only make objects move when I get upset.
Drake: (sitting) I wish I could make all this paperwork go away. Why is it so complicated to run a business?

Bob: Why so upset? With all those referrals from Freddie Flicks, your business is a smash. I can't believe we are in the office tonight without someone beating down the door.

Drake: Lucky at business, not so in love.

Bob: I thought we agreed on this "love" thing.

Drake: My mind tells me not to fall in love but, my cold heart longs for…

(Bell rings as door opens and Lacie Enters the Detective agency. Drake and Bob both stand as Lacie slowly approaches Drake)

Lacie: I wasn't sure I'd find you here. I've come by several times, but you are always closed.

Drake: I've been busy, and I keep late hours.

Lacie: Did you have time to see the movie?

Drake: Yes. It was, good. You were excellent but the guy who played the vampire? Why does everyone try to fake a foreign accent? Can't a vampire be from somewhere that doesn't have an accent?

Lacie: (looking around she notices the second desk) Oh, you got a partner. "Bob" (Reads name tag on desk)

Drake: HE's more of a silent partner. Never really here yet, it's like he's always here.

Bob: Very funny.

Lacie: Oh, I guess that's nice.

Drake: And you, you are doing fine?

Lacie: Yes. But I just wanted to…

Drake: (stands and moves around to Lacie) Yes?

Lacie: I wanted to stop by and tell you, that night on the set (Pause) I know what you are!

Drake: (Gets closer to Lacie, starts with accent like when practicing movie scene) No one really knows what I am, (changes to his normal voice) not behind this, this, mask of a man.

Lacie: Everything you said to me is it a lie? I suppose you've had many loves.

Drake: Yes, I have, you might as well know. How could I not have loved? I have been alive for five-hundred years.

Lacie: I suppose they are all dead now.

Drake: Yes.

Lacie: Did you kill them?

Drake: Only for the sake of mercy, when they were sick, dying.

Lacie: Do you have someone now?

Drake: Not for a long time. I got tired of falling in love and watching it fade away. (Takes Lacie's hands) That is why you must understand how special you are for me to take that chance again.

Lacie: You don't kill people now do you?

Drake: (Laughs) No, I have a way to get what I need that doesn't involve killing. I am helping people.

Lacie: Like you helped me?

Drake: Yes.

(Long Pause as Drake and Lacie stare into each other's eyes.)

Bob: Oh, for crying out loud would you just kiss her!

(Drake and Lacie kiss)

Lacie: I'm done with showbiz.

Drake: (Looks at the paperwork on his desk) I could use some help around here.

Lacie: You would let me help you?

Drake: Yes, of course. I am planning on being open for a long time.

(Lacie turns and eyes Bob's desk and Bob starts shaking his head)

Bob: Don't even think about it lady.

Drake: We can get you your own desk. Are you sure you are okay working with—a vampire?

Lacie: I'm not just working with a vampire. I'm in love with one.

Drake: And you are okay with it?

Lacie: Of course. I've fallen in love with a vampire and I know exactly what I'm doing. I saw it in a movie.

(Drake and Lacie Embrace, hopefully audience applauds)

Bob: Aren't you going to tell her about me.

Drake: No, Bob, I think she's had enough excitement for a while.

Lacie: What's that?

Drake: Nothing, dear. I said we've had enough excitement for a while. We should close for the night.

Lacie: What are we going to do tomorrow?

Drake: Well, tomorrow we are planning a blood drive.

(The End)

Director notes:

1) The audience isn't supposed to know character "Bob" is a ghost until the story unfolds
2) Drake uses his powers to turn into a bat when he needs to get around. Use of a "bat" prop with the actual actor flying it around is recommended
3) Drake uses fake blood drives to get his supply and the first scene starts out with him pulling in the sign. He disguises this blood in in juice boxes. "It's my own blend."
4) The character "Freddie Flicks" can be cast as male or female.

THE NEW MINISTER

Louis Paul DeGrado

CHAPTER ONE
ASSIGNMENT

Bishop Rinaldo stirred at his desk as the phone rang waking him from a light sleep. He reached across and his left hand brought the receiver to his ear as he heard a panicked voice at the other end.

"The man you sent us is dead," an elevated masculine voice said.

"Mister Duran, is that you?" Bishop Rinaldo asked.

"Yes, it's me."

"Reverend Carter is dead, are you sure?"

"Yes, there's no doubt. He was not who we needed. I told you we needed someone strong-willed, with focus and resolution. Our entire town is now at risk. What do you intend to do?"

"I have just the man for you. I will send him right away," Bishop Rinaldo said.

"You better pick someone who is up to the task. Lives are at stake."

Bishop Rinaldo reached across his desk to a file recently placed in his inbox. He opened it and looked through the description. "I think I have just the man for the job."

"We need help now! How soon can he be here?" Mister Duran asked.

"Now, hold on," Bishop Rinaldo said. "You got yourselves into this."

"I know that. But our predecessors made a commitment to help, and you have not provided a way out of this. Are you going to help us or not?"

"I will have him there in two days."

The other end of the line went silent. Bishop Rinaldo pushed a button to get a dial tone and dialed another number.

"Hello, you've reached the rectory, Father Michael speaking."

"Father Michael," Bishop Rinaldo said, "I need you to tell Father Gerald Arriaga that I need to speak with him immediately. Tonight, if possible."

"I will send him to you," Father Michael said.

Bishop Rinaldo hung up the phone and continued to look over the file in front of him. Father Gerald Arriaga was a recent transfer from oversees and he had not assigned him a parish. It seemed he had a mission now and a perfect one for his background; "He studied demonology abroad," he said as he opened his bottom right desk drawer and pulled out a flask of brandy and took a drink. "How convenient that he is here at this moment."

A knock came at the door.

"Please, come in," Bishop Rinaldo said and stood to greet Father Arriaga. "Sorry it's so dark in here, I've been resting." At five feet, ten inches tall, Bishop Rinaldo was not a small man. He was surprised that in front of him stood a man who was at least six foot, well built, and in his forties at best. A face with deep set, brown eyes, a chiseled chin, and black well-trimmed hair looked at him and Bishop Rinaldo suddenly felt he was the lower in status.

"Bishop Rinaldo," Father Arriaga said, "it's a pleasure to meet you." His hand came out and Bishop Rinaldo shook it in the formal greeting. "Is there something wrong?"

"Please, be seated," Bishop Rinaldo said and gestured to a leather, chalus chair in front of his desk. He returned to the chair behind his desk. "Nothing is wrong. It's just, I was reading your file and, with all the travel and experience you've had, I suppose I expected someone..."

"Older?" Father Arriaga said.

"Yes," Bishop Rinaldo said.

"I hope that doesn't affect the assignment you have for me."

"Not at all. In fact, I am glad to see you are in good health. Tell me, are you enjoying your stay here?"

"Yes, I never knew Colorado was so beautiful. The mountains are breathtaking."

"You have never been to Colorado before?" Bishop Rinaldo asked.

"Yes," Father Arriaga replied. "Only the south-eastern part where it is much flatter."

"Is there a reason you have not been settled at a parish and remained?" Bishop Rinaldo asked.

"I have always been put on special assignments; none of which have allowed me the pleasure of remaining in one place for long," Father Arriaga said.

"Does that bother you?"

"Not at all."

"I've been told you are a problem solver," Bishop Rinaldo said.

"Yes, I've been called that."

Bishop Rinaldo picked up the file on Father Arriaga and glanced at it. "I also see that you studied demonology,"

"Yes, I found it interesting," Father Arriaga said.

"I have a problem with a small parish in Dyersville and I need someone to go there immediately. It's a small, mountain town that would be a perfect place for you to witness more of Colorado's beauty. These small towns are where we have some of our most committed and faithful patrons. The city council there has always supported our church and its efforts. We must protect them."

"Protect them?" Father Arriaga asked. "I'm not sure I've heard it put that way before."

"Let's just say they have certain beliefs there that your background in demonology might help you understand. You will learn more about what I am referring too after you've arrived. The community church is small, adequate for the task. There are no accommodations so you will be staying with a host family, the Duran's. When you arrive in town, Paul Duran will greet you at the church."

"Is there currently no one at the parish?" Father Arriaga asked.

Bishop Rinaldo hesitated before he answered. "There was a Father Carter there. He had a crisis of faith. Perhaps the remote location had something to do with it." He stood causing Father Arriaga to do the same as he headed toward the door. "I need you there as soon as possible."

"I can leave tomorrow," Father Arriaga said.

"Good," Bishop Rinaldo said. "I will arrange transportation."

"Will there be anything else?" Father Arriaga asked.

Bishop Rinaldo looked to the floor before responding. "You will need to discover what is there on your own terms, Father Arriaga. Once you do, I am hoping some of what you referred too as 'problem solving' skills will be of use. If not, I can find someone to replace you if you wish to leave."

CHAPTER TWO
MEETING FAITH

Father Arriaga observed closely from the backseat of the car he rode in as he entered Dyersville. The town before him included one grocery store, a small school that, according to the sign, combined all grades. One gas station and a main street lined with businesses ended at the modest church. Though only a few houses were in town, he could see many houses lining the hillside sticking out of the mountainous forest. These houses, large and modern he noted, were not those of a poor, mountain town but spoke of wealth.

"I would make sure you stock up before winter," the silver-haired driver who'd met him in Denver told Father Arriaga as they arrived at the church.

"Once the snow sets in, it's almost impossible to get up here. And coming down the mountain is impossible."

"I'll keep that in mind," Father Arriaga said.

"You sure you want me to leave you off at the church?" The driver said. "I was instructed to take you to the Duran's house."

"The church will be fine," Father Arriaga said. "I want to see it before I go anywhere else. I can call the Duran's when I'm ready."

"You'll have to use the phone in the church," the driver said. "There's no cell service here. Well, here we are."

The driver carried Father Arriaga's bag into the church and then parted. Father Arriaga looked around the church which contained modern, padded seats instead of pews and a brightly lit alter area. The microphone, sound system and lighting were all state of the art. "Not a town in financial need," he said to himself.

He went to the alter and the podium where he would deliver his messages and looked out at the empty seats in front of him. He paused for a moment and visualized giving a sermon.

He went into the small ready room to the side of the alter where priests kept their garments and sacraments. It was in the small room where he found a desk and browsed around. He browsed through the side drawers only to find a few files of counseling sessions.

He opened the middle drawer and it appeared empty until he started to close it and it jammed. Upon examining it, he found a journal lodged between the back of the drawer and the desk.

Father Arriaga moved the drawer back and forth several times and worked the journal into a position where he could reach it and pried the small book out. He opened it to find it was a log from Father Carter, the previous minister. As he read the journal, he grew concerned by the story the writing told.

"I have found an evil here more real than I ever imagined," Father Carter wrote. "I was not prepared to have my faith tested so, but the town has confided in me secrets; unimaginable secrets of a pact made to save it from destruction. Although warned, I have decided that this cannot continue, and I have chosen to confront this sacrilege."

The writing stopped and there were no entries after this. Father Arriaga heard the door open and footsteps in the church. He put the journal back in the drawer and headed out through the side door and found a tall, dark-haired, middle-aged man in the church. He wore designer jeans and a dress shirt with a sport coat.

"Father Arriaga?" the man before him asked.

"Yes, I am he," Father Arriaga said. "Mister Duran?"

"You can call me Paul," he said and put out his hand.

The man who presented himself was dressed in a brown, causal suit without a tie, stood a good foot shorter than Father Arriaga but was in shape. He noticed he had city hands, callous free and soft.

"Did you just arrive?"

"I've been here a few hours," Father Arriaga said.

"The Bishop acted quickly then," Paul said.

"Was that important?"

"What did he tell you about our town?"

"Just that the previous minister had left; something about a crisis of faith and that you had requested someone to fill in." He decided not to mention anything further and let the rest be revealed to him by the actions of those he would meet. Besides, Bishop Rinaldo hadn't given any direct information, just a comment about his skills. He was sure to learn the town's secret soon enough.

"Well, I guess I better fill you in," Paul said. "But not before you had dinner and we get you settled. There's no place to stay here at the church so we've set up a room at the house. Is that your only bag?"

"Yes," Father Arriaga said.

"Sworn to poverty," Paul said. "I don't know how you do it."

The two men exited the church and went to a gray jeep. Paul put the bags in the back and the two headed out of town.

"Tell me about your town," Father Arriaga said.

"We are a rural people," Paul said. "A small community, but tight in our values. The town was founded in the eighteen-hundreds, a mining town. It nearly died out in the early nineteen-hundreds. Several fires struck the area. That along with the mines drying up led people to start leaving. Only a few families remained."

"Yes, I've heard about the old mining towns in Colorado. Some of them have found new life with the casinos and gambling," Father Arriaga said. His comment drew a stern look.

"No gambling in this town," Paul said. "There's always something bad that follows that type of industry. We might be small and sometimes barely getting by as a town, but we have values."

"I meant no offense," Father Arriaga said. In the back of his mind he was thinking about the journal he found at the church and couldn't help but wonder what evil Father Carter was speaking of when he wrote his final entry.

"Here we are," Paul said pulling into a large, two-story wood house that looked modern with its stained wood and huge windows. There were multiple cars parked in the driveway leading to the house.

"Do a lot of people live here?" Father Arriaga asked.

"No. Just my family is here. We invited some of the town council to meet you," Paul said.

"Oh, I wish I'd had time to clean up a little."

"You look fine, Father," Paul said.

Paul parked the car and the two men went inside. Father Arriaga met three families that were on the town council and Paul's wife, a thin, blonde woman named Debra. They ate dinner that included fresh trout from the area, baked potatoes, salad, and rolls. Father Arriaga answered questions when asked and spoke about his travels. Most of his time he tried to listen and observe. The people around the table were friendly and welcoming; happy that he arrived so soon.

After dinner, he went into the living room where the conversations continued. He noticed family pictures on the large mantle of the fireplace, and it was his question that darkened the mood of the room.

"I see you have a daughter, Paul. Is she away at college? She looks about that age."

Multiple eyes in the room looked to the floor as though searching for a lost pair of contacts or money and the rest turned to Paul who shifted his weight from leg to leg but didn't answer.

"Well, we should be going," one of the men said and then the others followed until all the families left, leaving Father Arriaga alone with Paul and his wife.

"I'm sorry," Father Arriaga said. "Did I say something wrong?"

"Oh, no," Debra said. "Why don't you have a seat in the living room. Would you like something to drink? Brandy, wine, beer?"

"No, I'm fine," Father Arriaga said.

Debra left and brought back a glass of wine for herself and what appeared to be a whiskey for her husband who stood by the mantle looking at the picture that included the girl Father Arriaga assumed was their daughter.

"I should wait until you've had a good night rest to tell you," Paul said as he drank half of his whiskey. "The truth is, we are running out of time to save her."

"Your daughter?"

"Yes," Paul said and finished his drink, putting the glass down on the coffee table, he took a seat in a leather recliner. "You better sit down."

Father Arriaga took a seat on the brown, all leather couch while Debra sat at the other end.

"Please don't judge us in what I am about to tell you. We are a God-fearing people and we've done what we thought we had to do. Everyone in the town knows and everyone has agreed to keep it a secret. What I'm about to reveal to you has been a curse on our town for decades. That's why we asked for you, a man of stronger faith. Father Carter, well, he wasn't up to it."

Father Arriaga leaned forward. "Tell me. What is it that has you so worried?"

Paul's eyes shifted to the empty glass and then back to Father Arriaga. His eyes were fixed forward when he asked, "Do you believe in demons?"

Louis Paul DeGrado

CHAPTER THREE
THE DARKNESS IN THE BASEMENT

Paul sat in his chair and stared forward as he recounted a story of how the town elders, faced with an out of control fire and certain doom made a pact with a demon to save the town from destruction. The deal was that the demon could possess a member of the community and exist among them. However, once the town was saved, the person the demon possessed was thrown into a cage and the local minister tried to exercise the demon only to fail.

The demon took it's revenge by drying up the mines and causing the town to descend into poverty. The church managed to control the demon and keep it from affecting the community any further but it still managed to possess a member of each generation and families fled the area never to return.

"The last person the demon possessed was my mother," Paul said. "The girl in the picture is our daughter, Susan. When my mother passed, the demon went into my daughter. That was just a few weeks ago."

"Did Father Carter know about all of this?" Father Arriaga asked.

"Yes, but he didn't truly accept it. You see, my mother was a strong woman and fought the demon. Most of the time she went about her business and seemed normal; no one could tell she was possessed. When she died and the demon moved into my daughter, things changed; her faith wasn't as deep, and the demon has all but taken control of her. Father Carter tried to help, but he wasn't strong enough."

"So, he left?" Father Arriaga asked.

"Not exactly," Paul said. "It's kind of hard to explain."

"I see," Father Arriaga said. He decided to give up on finding Father Carter's where abouts and focus on the girl. "Where is your daughter now?"

"We keep her in the basement," Paul said. "You should really get a good night sleep before you meet her."

"I'm fine," Father Arriaga said. "I wish to see her now." He stood causing Debra and Paul to stand. "I insist."

"Please, help her," Debra said.

"I don't think he believes us," Paul said.

"Why would I doubt you?" Father Arriaga asked.

"Very well, come with me," Paul said, and the two men headed down a hallway to a solid door that was padlocked. Paul took out a key and opened the door. "If you don't mind, I'm going to stay up here. I don't think I can bear to see her right now."

Father Arriaga put his hand on Paul's shoulder. "I don't mind, now I'm glad I got here so fast."

"Be careful," Paul said. "She lies."

"It's okay, I've dealt with this before," Father Arriaga said and headed down the wooden staircase. He emerged into a well-lit large, single room basement. In the room was a ping-pong table, air hockey, and foosball table. In the corner of the room, by a karaoke machine, the girl from the picture, young with brunette hair, sat alone. In front of the chair on the floor was a significant pile of ash.

"Hello, Father Arriaga," the girl said.

"Hello, Susan. Am I speaking with Susan?" Father Arriaga asked.

"Of course, I'm Susan. You don't believe all that stuff they told you about demons, do you?"

"How do you know what I was told?" Father Arriaga asked.

"The vents allow sound to travel," Susan said.

"Why would I doubt them?" Father Arriaga said.

"You think demons are real? You're as crazy as everyone else around here. At least untie me so I can get out of here. What kind of priest would allow a girl's father to keep her tied up in a basement?"

Father Arriaga approached the girl and could see she was strapped to the chair. He examined the pile of ashes on the floor. He knelt and made the sign of the cross and said a prayer.

"Oh no, you know." Susan said.

"Yes," Father Arriaga said and stood. "Why did you do this to Father Carter," he looked at the pile of ashes.

"He tried to make me leave," Susan said. "I don't want to leave."

"Why don't you want to leave?" Father Arriaga asked. "You don't belong here."

"I made a deal and as long as the town is here, I get to be here, see," Susan said.

"I've heard about this deal," Father Arriaga said as he walked around the chair. "Why did you pick Susan?"

"I didn't," Susan said. "The family had a choice. When grandma died, I needed a host. None of them wanted to allow me in, so I told them I would pick Susan. She was too young to resist and I knew she would be around for a long time. They let it happen."

"That wasn't nice of them," Father Arriaga said. He continued to move around Susan.

"I agree," Susan said. "I will make you a deal preacher."

"What is that?"

"You think this family brought you here to protect them, they didn't. They brought you here because I told them too. I told them I wanted a stronger vessel to inhabit; one that would allow me access to certain places."

"I have been baptized in the name of the trinity. You cannot inhabit me. I am protected," Father Arriaga said.

"I can if you allow me entry."

"Why me?" Father Arriaga asked.

"I need someone who could get me places only a priest can go," Susan said.

"Why did you not try this with Father Carter?"

"I did. He was too weak to take the bargain."

"Bargain?"

"For the girl," Susan said. "His soul for the salvation of the girl. Father Carter thought he could break the deal. He didn't really understand."

"Why would you want me? I would be a terrible host. We wouldn't agree on much," Father Arriaga said.

"I have questions that need answers," Susan said.

"Questions?"

"Why I am what I am. Does He," she glanced to the ceiling, "really exist."

"That is fascinating," Father Arriaga said. "I never thought I would see this day."

"You don't believe me, do you?"

"Why wouldn't I believe you?"

"Father Carter didn't, not at first. He thought this was mental illness; brought on by the family's superstitions. You don't believe demons are real, that I am really possessing this girl. You probably think it's puberty, adolescence."

"Actually, I fully believe," Father Arriaga said. "You would be surprised how much we have in common."

"What are you talking about?" Susan said. "What could we possibly have in common?"

Father Arriaga kept circling Susan as he spoke. "You said people don't believe in you, that they don't believe your kind exists right?"

"Yes," Susan said.

"Well, I have the same problem," Father Arriaga said. "People don't believe in me either, not my kind anyway."

"You're kind?" Susan said. "Would you stop circling you're making me dizzy."

Father Arriaga came to a stop in front of Susan and went down on one knee to face her directly. His eyes became a bright, white light as he reached out and grasped Susan's hands. A halo of gold light appeared above his head as he spoke. "I will answer one question for you, so you know."

"I don't believe it," Susan said. "You're real?"

"Yes, and so is He. Your kind have betrayed His law of life; that you are not above others, and it is not yours to take. That is your question and I have answered. Now, I command you to leave."

"What about the deal?" Susan said.

"The deal is over. You take your revenge, but you cannot take this girl," Father Arriaga said. "Don't test me."

Susan's head tilted downward, and she went limp.

The halo over Father Arriaga's head disappeared and his eyes returned to normal. He stood and went to the back of the chair. He undid the straps that held Susan and lifted her out of the chair.

"I've got you," Father Arriaga said and carried her up the stairs.

"Is she?" Debra said as Father Arriaga came through the basement door.

"She needs water," Father Arriaga said as he sat her down on the couch.

Debra left the room as Paul knelt by his daughter.

"How can I ever thank you?" Paul said.

"We need to leave, now," Father Arriaga said. "Does your school have a bus?"

"Yes," Paul said. "Just one."

"That will do," Father Arriaga said. "I need every child in town on that bus in the next hour. We have very little time."

"You think the demon will come for them?" Paul asked.

"No, but we should take precautions."

"Yes, of course," Paul said. "We probably need to get her to the medical center. I'll start the car." He left the house as Debra came back with a wet rag and put it on Susan's head. Susan moved back and forth and drank some water as she opened her eyes.

"Mom?"

"Yes, Susan, it's me." Debra said.

"We need to leave, now," Father Arriaga said and helped Susan stand.

"You," Susan said as she looked to Father Arriaga. "You were in my dream."

"Yes," Father Arriaga said. "And just like in your dream, you must listen to me now."

"I don't know if we should go anywhere tonight," Paul said as he entered the living room. "There's one hell of a storm out there. I've never seen lightning like that, not this close to winter."

"We need to go, now," Father Arriaga said as he escorted Susan to the door and into the jeep outside. Debra and Paul followed.

They entered the jeep with Susan and her mother in the back and Father Arriaga in the passenger's seat as Paul Drove. They started to pull away when a bolt of lightning struck the house causing it to explode in flames.

"My God," Paul said.

"You can say that" Father Arriaga said.

As they drove down the main street, many buildings were ablaze from lightning strikes and the trees surrounding the town were on fire.

"I don't know if we can make it to the emergency center," Paul said.

"We can't," Father Arriaga said. "We need to get to the school. Keep going, it's no longer safe here. Once we get to the school, we will leave town tonight."

The car sped down main street and to the edge of town when suddenly, a large tree full of fire fell in front of them and blocked the road. Paul slammed on the brakes

"Lord, forgive these two, they did not know how to deal with the evil of their kin," Father Arriaga said. "This family is asking for a second chance. Pray with me."

Paul, Debra, and Susan all prayed as Father Arriaga left the vehicle. He went to the tree and moved it out of the way. When he returned to the car, the family was silent.

"I suggest we go," Father Arriaga said.

"Yes, of course. Go," Paul said as he and his family continued down the road to the school.

"What the hell is going on?" a man yelled at Paul and Father Arriaga when they exited the car at the school. "The entire town is on fire."

"This is principal Meyers," Paul said.

"Yes, we met at dinner," Father Arriaga said.

"Are the children loaded on the bus?" Father Arriaga said.

"No, most of them are in the school," Meyers said.

"We need them in the bus now!" Father Arriaga said and the principal turned and ran to the school. Soon, a row of children followed and entered the bus.

"The driver is not here," Paul said. "And we are missing some of the kids."

"We will have to take what we can get. We are out of time," Father Arriaga said. "I will drive." He looked at Paul. "You and the rest of the parents can follow, but I cannot guarantee that I can get you out. It was you who made a deal with the demon, not these children."

"Let's go then," Paul said as he and Debra yelled out to the other parents to get in their cars and follow.

Father Arriaga entered the bus and started the engine. He turned to the children. "Anyone know a good song that everyone can sing?"

A kid sang out and the others joined in as Father Arriaga hit the gas and moved with haste down the road. He watched behind him as lightning struck and school building lit up. Then, one by one the cars behind him were struck till only the bus remained and continued its path down the road to salvation.

Somewhere in Colorado, a town once named Dyersville, consumed by flame, no longer exists.

The END.

Louis Paul DeGrado

Now that you've finished
Now that you're through
Don't let the fear
Take hold of you
Don't worry about grave robbers
Vampires or demons
Or other creatures of the night
Just say your prayers
and sleep tighty tight
but don't rest before
you check under the bed
in the closet
and lock the front door

See More at

www.Literarylou.com

Home of Author

Louis Paul DeGrado

Made in the USA
Middletown, DE
11 August 2024